Also by Tom McCarthy

SATIN ISLAND

SATIN
ISLAND

A NOVEL

Tom McCarthy

Alfred A. Knopf

New York · 2015

THIS IS A BORZOI BOOK
PUBLISHED BY ALFRED A. KNOPF

All rights reserved. Published in the United States by
Alfred A. Knopf, a division of Random House LLC, New York,
a Penguin Random House company.

www.aaknopf.com

Knopf, Borzoi Books, and the colophon
are registered trademarks of Random House LLC.

Library of Congress Cataloging-in-Publication Data
McCarthy, Tom, [date]
  Satin Island : a novel / Tom McCarthy.
      pages   cm
  ISBN 978-0-307-59395-5 (hardback) —
  ISBN 978-1-101-87468-4 (eBook)   1. Mind and reality—
  Fiction.   2. Psychological fiction. I. Title.
    PR6113.C369S38 2015
    823'.92—dc23

                                        2014023461

Jacket design by Peter Mendelsund

Manufactured in the United States of America
First Edition

For Matt Parker

Outside, like the cry of space, the traveller
perceives the whistle's distress. "Probably,"
he persuades himself, "we are going through a
tunnel—*the epoch*—the last long one, snaking
under the city to the all-powerful train station
of the virginal central palace, like a crown."

—*Mallarmé*

SATIN ISLAND

I.

I.I Turin is where the famous shroud is from, the one showing Christ's body supine after crucifixion: hands folded over
genitals, eyes closed, head crowned with thorns. The image
isn't really visible on the bare linen. It only emerged in the late
nineteenth century, when some amateur photographer looked
at the negative of a shot he'd taken of the thing, and saw the
figure—pale and faded, but there nonetheless. Only in the
negative: the negative became a positive, which means that
the shroud itself was, in effect, a negative already. A few decades
later, when the shroud was radiocarbon dated, it turned out to
come from no later than the mid-thirteenth century; but this
didn't trouble the believers. Things like that never do. People
need foundation myths, some imprint of year zero, a bolt that
secures the scaffolding that in turn holds fast the entire architecture of reality, of time: memory-chambers and oblivion-
cellars, walls between eras, hallways that sweep us on towards
the end-days and the coming whatever-it-is. We see things
shroudedly, as through a veil, an over-pixellated screen. When
the shapeless plasma takes on form and resolution, like a fish
approaching us through murky waters or an image looming

into view from noxious liquid in a darkroom, when it begins
to coalesce into a figure that's discernible, if ciphered, we can
say: *This is it, stirring, looming,* even if it isn't really, if it's all just
ink-blots.

I.2 One evening, a few years ago, I found myself stuck in
Turin. Not in the city, but the airport: Torino-Caselle. Lots
of other people did too: nothing was taking off. The phrase
Await Announcements multiplied, stacked up in columns on the
information screens, alternately in English and Italian. What
was causing the delay was a rogue aeroplane, some kind of
private jet, which, ignoring all instructions, was flying in idiosyncratic patterns over Southern England and the Channel;
which meant that no other planes could penetrate that swath
of airspace; which in turn, via the series of switches and trans-
fers and reroutings that had been put in place to deal with the
whole situation, had spread a huge delay-cloud over Europe.
So I sat, like everyone else, sifting through airline- and airport-
pages on my laptop for enlightenment about our quandary—
then, when I'd exhausted these, clicking through news sites
and social pages, meandering along corridors of trivia, generally killing time.

I.3 That's when I read about the shroud. When I'd done reading about that I started reading about hubs. Torino-Caselle is a
hub-airport. There was a page on their website explaining what

this is. Hub-airports are predominantly transfer points, rather than destinations in and of themselves. The webpage showed a diagram of a rimless wheel, with spokes of different lengths all leading to the centre, such that communion between any two spots on the wheel's surface area was possible despite no direct line connecting these. It looked like Jesus' crown, with all its jutting prongs. A link took me to an external page that explained how the hub-model was used in fields ranging from freight to distributed computing. Soon I was reading about flanges, track sprockets and bearings in bicycle construction. Then I clicked on *freehub*. These incorporate splines—mating features for rotating elements—and a ratchet mechanism, built into the hub itself (rather than adjacent to or above it, as in previous, non-freehub models), whose temporary disengagement permits coasting.

I.4 To a soundtrack, incongruous, of looped, recorded messages and chimes, a fruit-machine's idle-tune, snatches of other people's conversations and the staggered, intermittent hiss, quieter or louder, of steam-arms at espresso bars dotted about the terminal, a memory came to me: of freewheeling down a hill as a child, riding my second bike. It wasn't a specific memory of riding down the hill on such-and-such a day: more a generic one in which hundreds of hill-descents, accumulated over two or three years, had all merged together. Where my first bike had had a footbrake, activated by the pedal, this one, fitted with a handbrake instead, allowed backpedalling. This struck me, I remembered, as nothing short of miraculous. That you could move one way while rotating the crank in the opposite direction contravened my fledgling understanding not only of motion but also of time—as though this, too, could be laced with a contraflow lodged right inside its core. Whenever I hurtled, backpedalling, down the hill, I'd feel exhilaration, but also vertigo—vertigo tinged with a slight nausea. It wasn't an entirely pleasant feeling. Recalling the manoeuvre now reproduced—in the crowded terminal, in my head and stomach—the same awkward sense of things being out of sync, out of whack.

1.5 Around me and my screen, more screens: of other laptops, mobiles, televisions. These last screens had tickers scrolling across them, text whose subjects included the air delay in which I was caught up. Behind the tickers, news footage was running. One screen showed highlights of a football game. Another showed the aftermath of a marketplace truck bombing somewhere in the Middle East, the type of scene you always see in this kind of report: hysterical, blood-spattered people running about screaming. One of these people, a man who looked straight at the camera as he ran towards it, wore a T-shirt that showed Snoopy lounging on his kennel's roof, the word *Perfection* hovering in the air above him. Then the scene gave over to an oil spill that had happened somewhere in the world that morning, or the night before: aerial shots of a stricken offshore platform around which a large, dark water-flower was blooming; white-feathered sea birds, filmed from both air and ground, milling around on pristine, snowy shorelines, unaware of the black tide inching its way towards them; and, villain of the piece, shot by an underwater robot, a broken pipe gushing its endless load into the ocean.

1.6 My phone beeped and vibrated in my jacket. I took it out and read the message I'd received. It came from Peyman. Peyman was my boss. It said: We won. That was it. Two boys ran past me; one fell down; his brother jolted to a halt, backtracked a few paces and roughly pulled him to his feet; they ran on. I looked up again at the television monitor on which the football game was showing. The goal I'd seen a moment earlier was replaying in slow motion. The ball's trajectory, the arc it followed as it cleared defenders' heads and keeper's hands, the backspin of its hexagons and stars, the sudden buckle and eruption of the net's neat grid as the ball hit it—this sequence now aligned itself with these words sent to me by Peyman: We won. I looked at the screen's upper corner, where the scoreline was displayed, to see which teams were playing. Barcelona and Bayern Munich. I texted him back: Who won what? Company won Project contract, he responded half a minute later. This I understood. The Company was our company, Peyman's company, the company I worked for. The Project was the Koob-Sassen Project; we'd been going after the contract for some time. Good, I texted. The answer came more quickly this time: Good? That's it? I deliberated for a few seconds, then sent back a new message: Very good. His next text crossed with mine: You still stuck in transit? I confirmed this. Me too, Peyman eventually informed me; in Vienna. Come see me tomorrow a.m. Then a message came from Tapio. Tapio was Peyman's right-hand man. Company won KSP contract, it said. Two more, from other colleagues, followed in quick succession, both conveying the same news. The effects of my chance exposure to this football game lingered after I'd read these; so it seemed to me that Bayern Munich's striker, roaring with delight towards the stands, was rejoicing not for his own team and fans but rather for us; and it even seemed that the victim with the Snoopy shirt on, as he ran screaming towards the camera, was celebrating the news too: from his ruined market with its standard twisted metal and its blood, for us.

I.7 Now my laptop started ringing: someone was Skyping me. *JoanofArc,* the caller-ident box read. I recognized the handle: it belonged to a woman named Madison, whom I'd met two months previously in Budapest. I clicked to accept. Can you hear me? Madison's voice asked. I said that I could. Activate your camera, the voice instructed me. I did this. Madison appeared to me at the same time. She asked me where I was. I told her. She told me that she'd been in Torino-Caselle Airport too, in 2001. What brought you here? I asked her, but my question seemed to get lost in the relay; she didn't answer it, at any rate. Instead, she asked when I'd be back in London. Her face, on my screen, jumped in small cascades of motion from one pool of stillness to another. I don't know, I said. I popped the news page open as I talked to her. The airspace lock-up was announced halfway down, adjacent to and in the same font-size as the marketplace truck bombing. Above it, slightly larger, the oil spill, with a sequence of photos showing tugs, oil-covered men wrestling with grips and winches, those black-ringed outlying islands, the giant oil-flower and so forth. The editor had chosen a "fade" effect to link the shots together, rather than the more abrupt type of succession that recalls old slideshow carousels. It struck me as the right effect to use, aesthetically speaking.

1.8 The same two boys ran past me. Once more the small one's feet slipped out from under him: it must have been the angle as the floor rounded the row of seats—that, and the fact that the floor was polished. Once more his brother (if it was his brother) picked him up and they ran on. Madison asked once more when I'd be back. She said she needed ethnological attention. How so? I asked, sliding her screen back above the news page. I'm lacking, she began to tell me—but just then the audio dropped. Her face froze in mid-sentence too. Its mouth was open in an asymmetric, drooley kind of way, as though she'd lost control of its muscles following a stroke; her eyes had rolled upwards, so the pupils were half-hidden by the lids. A little circle span in front of her, to denote buffering. My screen stayed that way for a long, long time, while I gazed at it, waiting for the buffering to pass. It didn't: instead, a *Call Ended* message eventually replaced both face and circle.

I.9 I looked up, around the terminal. People who weren't clicking and scrolling their way, like me, through phones and laptops were grazing on the luxury items stacked up all about us. The more valuable of these were kept behind polished glass sheets whose surfaces reflected the lounge's other surfaces, so that the marketplace bomb-aftermath replayed across the pattern of a shawl, oil flowed and reflowed on a watch's face. The overlap between these various elements, and the collage-effect it created, was constant—but, as the hours wore on, the balance of the mixture changed. The luxury objects and their cases stayed the same, of course—but little by little, football highlights and truck bombing faded, clips of them growing shorter and less frequent; while, conversely, the oil spill garnered more and more screen time. It was obviously a big one. By midnight, those oil-drenched men I'd seen in the news-page photos were on the airport's TV screens as well—but moving now, laying floating booms, trying, without any apparent success, to herd and corral the flow of water-borne oil as it forked and turned and spread out. They looked like demoralized, tug-mounted cowboys whose black cattle, through sheer mass and volume, had mutinied, stampeded and grown uncontrollable. Other sequences simply showed oil-saturated water, dark and ponderous. It seemed to move, to swell and crest, at once more slowly and faster than water usually does—as though, just like the goal that by now had retreated to a single sport-bar TV set at my vision's edge, it had been filmed with high-end motion-capture cameras, the type that sharpen and amplify each frame, each moment, lifting it out of the general flow and releasing it back into this at the same time. I found this movement fascinating. I watched the images for hour after hour, my head rotating with them as they moved from screen to screen.

1.10 The man sitting beside me, noticing the rapt attention I was paying these pictures, tried at one point to spark up a conversation. Tutting disapprovingly in their direction, he opined that it was a tragedy. That was the word he used, of course: *tragedy*—like a TV pundit. I looked him up and down, scanning his get-up. He was wearing a suit but had removed his tie, and laid it, folded, on a wheel-mounted carry-on bag that stood beside him. He addressed me in English, but his accent was Eurozone: neither French nor Dutch nor German but a mishmash of all these and more, overlaid with ersatz, business-school American. I didn't answer at first. When I did, I told him that the word *tragedy* derived from the ancient Greek custom of driving out a sheep, or *tragos*—usually a black one—in a bid to expiate a city's crimes. He turned back to the screen and watched it with me for a while as though this shared activity now formed part of our dialogue, of our new friendship. But

I could feel he was upset not to have got the response that he'd expected. After a few minutes, he stood up, grasped the handle of the bag on which his tie was resting and walked off.

I.II I, for my part, stayed put, watching the crippled platform listing, the broken pipe gushing, the birds milling around, the oil-flower unfurling its petals, the dark water swelling and cresting, over and over again. I watched, as I said, for hour after hour; when no public screen was showing these scenes, I watched them on first one and then another of my private ones. They kept me utterly engrossed until, much later, in the small hours of the morning, the airspace unlocked and my flight was called. Nor did I leave them behind me then. When I had finally got airborne, and found my head slumped flat against the window as I slipped into a flecked and grainy sleep, oil seemed to lie around the very cloud-patches the wing-lights were illuminating: to lurk within and boost their volume, as though absorbed by them, and to seep out from them as well, in blobs and globules that hovered on their ledges, sat about their folds and crevasses, like so many blackened cherubs.

2.

2.I Me? Call me U. It's not my intention, here, to write about the Koob-Sassen Project—to give an exegesis, overview, whatever, of it. There are legal reasons for this: sub-clauses of contracts sitting in the drawers of cabinets that I always picture (and this, perhaps, is not unconnected to my sense of the Project itself, which I came to envision this way too) as made out of some smooth, post-metallic compound—epoxy, say, or Kevlar—although in reality they could just as well be aluminium, wooden, MDF or so on; stipulations protecting commercial, governmental and the level that comes one above that confidentiality; interdictions on virtually all types of disclosure. And anyhow, even if there weren't, would you actually want to hear about it? It is, it strikes me, in the general scale of things, a pretty boring subject. Don't get me wrong: the Project was important. It will have had direct effects on you; in fact, there's probably not a single area of your daily life that it hasn't, in some way or other, touched on, penetrated, changed; although you probably don't know this. Not that it was secret. Things like that don't need to be. They creep under the radar by being boring. And complex. Koob-Sassen involved many hook-ups, interfaces, transpositions—corporate to civic, supranational to local, analogue to digital and open to restricted and hard to soft and who knows what else. It was a project formed of many other projects, linked to many other projects— which renders it well-nigh impossible to say where it began and ended, to discern its "content," bulk or outline. Perhaps all projects nowadays are like that—equally boring, equally inscrutable. So even if I could, and if you wanted me to, shine a (no more than anecdotal) spotlight on specific moments of Koob-Sassen's early phases, letting the beam linger on those passages and segments where the Company's operations, or my own small, insignificant activities, intersected them, would this, in any way, illuminate the Whole? I doubt it.

2.2 What do I do? I am an anthropologist. Structures of kinship; systems of exchange, barter and gift; symbolic operations lurking on the flipside of the habitual and the banal: identifying these, prising them out and holding them up, kicking and wriggling, to the light—that's my racket. When these events (*events!* If you want those, you'd best stop reading now) took place, I found myself deployed not to some remote jungle, steppe or tundra, there to study hunter-gatherers and shamans, but to a business. Deployed there, what's more, not by the austere dictates of a Royal Anthropological Society or National University, but by the very business to which I'd been dispatched: I was the in-house ethnographer for a consultancy. The Company (let's continue to call it that) advised other companies how to contextualize and nuance their services and products. It advised cities how to brand and re-brand themselves; regions how to elaborate and frame regenerative strategies; governments how to narrate their policy agendas—to the press, the public and, not least, themselves. We dealt, as Peyman liked to say, in narratives.

2.3 When, in those days, you entered the Company's Central London premises, passing the frequently changing but perennially attractive staff who manned the reception desk, a lift would bear you up to several floors of conferencing rooms and viewing suites and studios. Separated from each other by floor-to-ceiling glass partitions on which lower-case letters in the Company's own, distinctive font were stenciled, these compartments ran on one into the next, creating an expansive vista in which sketches, diagrams and other such configurations of precious data, lying face-up on curved tabletops, pinned to walls or drawn on whiteboards or, occasionally (and this made the data seem all the more valuable, *fragile* even), on the glass itself, seemed to dialogue with one another in a rich and esoteric language, the scene conveying (deliberately, of course) the impression that this was not only a place of business but, beyond that, a hermetic zone, a zone of alchemy, a crucible in which whole worlds were in the mix. The same lift that bore you up here, though, bore me down to a glassless, brick-and-plaster basement, where my own office was situated.

2.4 The ventilation system. This deserves a book all of its own. It was cavernous and booming. The air-handling unit was housed in the basement with me—a series of grey boxes joined to one another like parts of a mechanical elephant, a sheet-metal supply-duct curling upwards from the front box forming its raised trunk. The coils, blowers, dampers, filters and so on that made up the boxes' entrails transmitted a constant hum and rattle that permeated the whole floor, mutating in pitch and frequency as the sound negotiated corners, bounced off walls, was sponged up and squeezed out again by carpets. Before it left the basement, the duct forked, then branched out further, the new branch-ducts leading to diffusers, grilles and registers that, in turn, fed air onwards to other floors, before return-ducts carried it back down again, along a central plenum, to the rectum of the elephant, to be re-filtered, re-damped, re-coiled, then trumpeted back out into the building once again. Sometimes, when someone on a higher floor spoke loudly while they happened to be standing next to a return-vent, their words carried to the space in which I found myself, like the voice of a ship's captain sending orders through a speaking tube down to the engine rooms—orders, though, whose content became scrambled, lost in the delivery. Other, vaguer voices hovered in the general noise—or if not voices, at least patterns, with their ridges and their troughs, their repetition frequencies, their cadences and codas. Sometimes these patterns took on visual forms, like those that so enchanted eighteenth-century scientists when they scattered salt on Chladni plates and, exposing these to various acoustic stimuli, observed the intricate designs

that ensued—geometric and symmetrical and so generally perfect that they seemed to betray a universal structure lurking
beneath nature's surface, only now beginning to seep through;
and I, too, in my basement, sometimes thought I saw, moving
in ripples on the surface of a long-cold coffee cup or in the
close-up choreography of dust-flecks jumping on an unwiped
tabletop, or even on the fleshy insides of my own drooped
eyelids, the plan, formula, solution—not only to the problem
with which I was currently grappling, but to it *all*, the whole
caboodle—before, waking with a jolt, I watched it all evapo-
rate, like salt in a quiet breeze.

2.5 When I returned from Turin, I slept for a couple of
hours, then showered, then made my way into the office. It was
a clear day, one of those crisp ones in winter when the sunlight
seems to penetrate the thin, cold air more sharply; the glass and
metal carapace of the Company building was flashing blue and
silver, as though laced with an electric charge. Inside, too, the
place seemed all charged up: people were moving briskly, with
a bounce and purpose to their gait. It was the Project contract,
of course, the Company's landing of it, that was generating this
excitement. The name Koob-Sassen was being spoken in the
lobby, in the lift, along the corridors; even when nobody was
speaking it, it seemed to hang about the air and speak itself.
Arriving in my room, I called up to Peyman's office on the fifth
floor, and was put through to Tapio. U., Tapio said; you're back.
He spoke in a robotic Finnish monotone, but still he seemed

surprised. Yes, I said. Peyman's not, he told me; he's still stuck in Vienna. (The airspace there, it turned out, was backed up much worse than it had been in Italy.) He'll be back tomorrow though, Tapio continued; come and see him then. He hung up, leaving me alone in my basement, disconnected and deflated.

2.6 On that day, of all days, I left the office early. Rather than go back to my flat, I went to Madison's. She lived in Westbourne Grove. On the tube on the way there, I picked up one of the free newspapers that lay about the seats. The front page carried an update on the oil spill. The containment booms hadn't worked; oil was, slowly but ineluctably, encroaching on those shorelines. The paper had reproduced a chart that showed the way the currents circulated in that particular spot: they moved in a large circle, or, to be precise, ellipse, one of whose elongated edges intersected the coast and at whose antipodal point the broken pipeline sat, uptake and delivery of its effluvia thereby rendered all the more intense and concentrated by its and the coast's perfectly corresponding positions on the circumference. (There were, ironically, stretches of blank ocean lying much closer to the pipeline that were unaffected.) Looking at the chart, its directional arrows, I thought of those two boys, those brothers or not-brothers: I pictured them still running, sliding, plying their oval loop—not in the airport anymore, but on some other floor, a kitchen's or a school refectory's or playground's. Flipping onwards through the paper, I found my attention caught by a small item halfway through. A parachutist had died jumping from a plane. His parachute had detached from him, and he'd plummeted to earth. Although just twenty-five, he'd been a seasoned parachutist, a core member of the club under whose auspices this fatal jump had taken place. Police were treating the death as suspicious.

2.7 I'd met Madison, as I've already mentioned, two months earlier, in Budapest. I'd been at a conference. She'd been there with some girlfriends. We'd got talking in the hotel bar. An anthropologist, she'd said; that's . . . exotic. Not at all, I'd replied; I work for an incorporated business, in a basement. Yes, she said, but . . . But what? I asked. Dances, and masks, and feathers, she eventually responded: that's the *essence* of your work, isn't it? I mean, even if you're writing a report on workplace etiquette, or how to motivate employees or whatever, you're seeing it all through a lens of rituals, and rites, and stuff. It must make the everyday all primitive and strange—no? I saw what she was getting at; but she was wrong. For anthropologists, even the exotic's not exotic, let alone the everyday. In his key volume *Tristes Tropiques,* Claude Lévi-Strauss, the twentieth century's most brilliant ethnographer, describes pacing the streets, all draped with new electric cable, of Lahore's Old Town sometime in the nineteen-fifties, trying to piece together, long after the event, a vanished purity—of local colour, texture, custom, life in general—from nothing but leftovers and debris. He goes on to describe being struck by the same impression when he lived among the Amazonian Nambikwara tribe: the sense of having come "too late"—although he knows, from having read a previous account of life among the Nambikwara, that the anthropologist (that account's author) who came here fifty years earlier, before the rubber-traders and the telegraph, was struck by that impression also; and knows as well that the anthropologist who, inspired by the account that Lévi-Strauss will himself write of this trip, shall come back in fifty more will be struck by it too, and wish—*if only!*—that he could have been here fifty years ago (that is, now, or, rather, then) to see what *he,* Lévi-Strauss, saw, or failed to see. This leads him to identify a "double-bind" to which all anthropologists, and anthropology itself, are, by their very nature, prey: the "purity" they crave is no more than a state in which all frames of comprehension, of interpretation and analysis, are lacking; once these are brought to bear, the mystery that drew the anthropologist towards his subject in the first place vanishes. I explained this to her; and she seemed, despite the fact that she was drunk, to understand what I was saying. Wow, she murmured; that's kind of fucked.

2.8 When I arrived at Madison's, we had sex. Afterwards, lying in bed, I asked her what she'd been doing in Turin. I wasn't in Turin, she answered; *you* were. But you were too, I said. No I wasn't, she replied. You told me that you had been once, I said—when we Skyped, just last night. I never said I'd been in Turin, she mumbled into her pillow; she was half asleep. She was silent for a few moments, and I thought she'd drifted off. After a while, though, she continued mumbling. I said, she told me, that I'd been in Torino-Caselle. Okay, I said, Torino-Caselle: what were you doing there? Waiting, she said, just like you were. What for? I asked. A plane, she said. What else do people wait for in an airport?

3.

3.1 My meeting with Peyman didn't take place all that week. He'd been delayed in Vienna for so long that by the time a flight became available his schedule had him in Seattle, so he'd flown straight there. This was annoying—beyond annoying: frustrating. In fact, his absence filled me with what I can only describe as anxiety. Not that his presence made you feel un-anxious, calm; far from it. The whole place ran on anxiety: it was Peyman's motor-oil, his generative fuel. But there's anxiety and anxiety. With the Project contract won, knowing the weight he attached to it, I, like everyone else in the Company, was now anxious to see Peyman and, through Peyman, to connect: either to some rich and stellar network that we pictured lying behind this name, Koob-Sassen; or, if not that, then at least to . . . something. Being near Peyman made you feel connected. In his absence, I spent the week wrapping up other briefs that I'd been working on: transcribing audio files, drawing up charts, tweaking documents, drifting around websites. Mostly drifting around websites.

3.2 What does an anthropologist working for a business actually *do*? We purvey cultural insight. What does that mean? It means that we unpick the fibre of a culture (ours), its weft and warp—the situations it throws up, the beliefs that under-pin and nourish it—and let a client in on how they can best get traction on this fibre so that they can introduce into the weave their own fine, silken thread, strategically embroider or detail it with a mini-narrative (a convoluted way of saying: sell their product). Ethnographers do field research, creating photo-montages out of single moments captured in a street or café; or they get sample citizens—teenagers, office workers, mums—to produce video-diaries for them, outlining their daily routines in intimate detail, confiding to the camera the desires, emo-tions, aspirations and so forth that visit them as they unload a dishwasher, lace up trainers, or sip foam through that little slit you get in plastic coffee-cup lids. It's about identifying and probing granular, mechanical behaviours, extrapolating from a sample batch of these a set of blueprints, tailored according to each brief—blueprints which, taken as a whole and cross-mapped onto the findings of more "objective" or empirical studies (quantitative analysis, econometric modeling and the like), lay bare some kind of inner social logic, which can be har-nessed, put to use. In essence it's not that much different from what soothsayers, ichthyomancers, did in ancient times: those wolfskin-clad men who moved from stone-age settlement to stone-age settlement, cutting fish open to tease wisdom from their entrails. The difference being, of course, that soothsayers were frauds.

3.3 Once, for a brief time, I was famous. My renown came in the wake of my first—and only—major academic study. The study's subject was club culture. For three years, in the nineties—my mid-to-late twenties—I spent a large portion of my waking (and sleeping) hours among clubbers. I took a barman job in Bagleys; spent off-nights at the Fridge, the Ministry of Sound, the Velvet Rooms and Turnmills; took poppers, speed, MDMA; the lot. By the end I was helping procure venues for illicit raves, helping direct crowds to these through coded messages put out on pirate radio stations, cellular networks and the array of whisper-lines that spring up around this type of dubious activity. I then spent two more years writing it all up. On my study's publication (first as a doctoral thesis, then, two years later, with me in my mid-thirties, as an actual book that real people could buy), what was generally found to be most notable about it wasn't the insight it afforded into the *demimonde* or "mindset" or whatever you want to call it of clubbers, but rather the book's frequent and expansive "asides" in which I meditated on contemporary ethnographic method and its various quandaries.

3.4 For example: I considered at great length the question of field. In classical anthropology, there's a rigid distinction between "field" and "home." Field's where you go to do your research, immersing yourself, sometimes at great personal risk, in a maelstrom of raw, unsorted happening. Home's where you go to sort and tame it: catalogue it, analyze it, transform it into something meaningful. But when the object of your study is completely interwoven with your own life and its rhythms, this distinction vanishes: Where (I asked, repeatedly) does home end and field begin? Or—and this problem follows from the last—I reflected on the anthropologist's relation to the figures known as his "informants." If these people's background and culture are at base no different from your own, and if these people are your friends—albeit ones who might (or then again, might not) know of your sidebar ethnographic carryings-on— then how should you interrogate them? What constitutes "interrogation" in the first place? In what way should it be staged? Does sex with a Lycra-miniskirted informant on your writing table at five a.m. when you're both tripping count? Does passing out with someone in a toilet? Then, in the train of that one—and I'm not skipping the solutions to these predicaments, these pickles, since I didn't provide any—comes the question of the anthropologist's *persona*. Since the necessary act of approaching the familiar as a stranger, of behaving— even to yourself—as if you didn't understand the situations that in fact you do, is an obvious contrivance; and since, conversely, *pretending* to understand them, at a profound, unmediated level, to think and believe and desire certain premises, propositions, objects and outcomes, for the purpose of attaining better access to the subculture you're infiltrating, is equally contrived; or, to flip it back the other way again, to *actually* think and believe and desire these, but to be forced nonetheless, in your role as anthropologist, to *pretend* you're being and doing what you really *are* being and doing—in brief, since all this shit entails a constant shifting of identities, a blurring of positions and perspectives, you end up lost in a kaleidoscope of masquerades, roles, general make-believe.

3.5 I wrote about all this. It made me famous—relatively speaking. Let's not get carried away. A famous anthropologist, even one with a real book out, is about as well-known as a third-division footballer. No, less: let's say an Olympic badminton player, or a reality-TV contestant from an unpopular show five years ago. And come to think of it, I'm even exaggerating the degree of fame my study brought me in my own field, let alone the world of letters. Rather than "made me famous," it would be more accurate to say that the book "garnered me some attention"—the odd public reading, the odd newspaper review; and, as they say, tomorrow's fish (unlike ichthyomancers) can't read. It was enough attention, though, to bring me onto Peyman's radar, there to beep, or throb, or do whatever things on radars do; which, in turn, prompted him to pluck me from the dying branches of academia and re-graft me inside the febrile hothouse of his company.

3.6 My colleague Daniel had his office next to mine down in the basement. From time to time, I'd poke my head in there to see what he was up to. He was a visual-culture guy. He'd trained as a film-maker, and turned out a couple of avant-garde shorts before Peyman had hired him. When I looked into his office on the Tuesday of that week, I found him sitting watching a film, projected onto his white wall. It showed, shot from above, a section of a city crammed with traffic. What city's that? I asked him. It didn't look like a British or a European one, or North American either: the colours were different, and the vehicles seemed more wild and battered. It's Lagos, he said. I shot it with Peyman a few months back. President Goodluck Jonathan lent us his own personal helicopter to go up in. Lagos, said Daniel, has the most amazing traffic jams in the world. You mean the worst? I asked him. No, not necessarily, he said; I mean the most amazing. Almost everything in Lagos is public transport: yellow buses, huge blue and red and brown trucks. The streets, he went on, aren't wide enough for them, so they wedge and squish together. Look, he said: this portion coming up is great. I watched the wall, the footage. He was right: it was pretty awesome. Chains of buses maybe seven or eight long, these rivers of bright yellow, were trying to push their way down arteries that were too narrow for them, while isolated blocks of other colours tried to break in from the sides, insert themselves into the chains. When they succeeded, sequences of alternation and progression started typing themselves out: it looked like those helix-maps of DNA. The wildest thing about it all, said Daniel, is that, in between all these trucks and buses, there are people. You can't see them from this high up, but they're there. Won't they get crushed? I asked (there wasn't any space between the vehicles). You'd think so, Daniel said—but they slink in and out between and underneath them, like silverfish. Legend has it they're dismantling them, these people—dismantling the vehicles and reassembling them too: the jam turns into an unending car market or pit stop. These bits you see curling above the road, he told me, pointing at some fern leaf–shaped outgrowths, are highway exits that lead nowhere—the thoroughfare was actually designed for a city where they drive on the left, not the right. The city to whom the designers originally submitted the plan rejected it, then the Nigerian Transport Ministry bought it on the cheap and didn't bother to flip it around; and so there are these dead-end exit-ramps that all the vehicle parts are laid out in, organized by colour. I followed his finger: above the main road, in the dead-end curls, lay expanded pools in which red turned into yellow, yellow into brown, brown into black. It's like a palette-menu, isn't it? he said. The whole city's like a painting, painting itself as you watch. I nodded; he was right. We sat in silence for a long time, watching.

3.7 I didn't meet with Peyman that week, but I met with my friend Petr. Petr worked for a big IT outfit, as a systems analyst. I'd never really understood what that entailed, although he'd told me several times. We met in a pub. He had a thyroid goiter. You could see it on his neck: it moved about beneath the skin while he was talking, like a second Adam's apple. His doctor, Petr told me, had decided that the goiter should be surgically removed. The removal was to be carried out in a couple of days. It was a small, routine procedure: he'd be in and out of hospital on the same day. But Petr didn't want to talk about his goiter: he wanted to discuss the Project. His firm was working on it too, like hundreds of others. He congratulated me on the Company's recent "sign-up to the Grand Metamorphosis." What will you actually be doing? he asked. I couldn't really answer him. I told him that Peyman was out of town, and that things would become much clearer once he came back—although, as I spoke these words, I doubted if they were in fact correct. Hey, Petr asked me: how's the Great Report coming along? Oh, you know, I said: it's finding its form. This seemed to satisfy him; he went back to talking about Koob-Sassen. It was a huge, ambitious scheme, he said, on the same scale as poldering and draining landmasses of thousands of square miles, or cabling and connecting an entire empire—and yet, he continued, the most remarkable thing about it was that, despite its massive scale, it would remain, in an everyday sense, to members of the general populace, invisible: there'd be no monuments, no edifices towering above cities, spanning countrysides, dotting coastlines and so on. It was a feat, rather, of what he called *network architecture*. He went on for a long time about networks, convergence, nodes and relays, interstices—it was very abstract. I found myself zoning out; by the third drink, I'd stopped listening to his words completely and was paying all my attention to the goiter just above his voice-box, to the way that, like Lagos's traffic, it squished and slid.

3.8 On the way home from meeting Petr, I picked up one of those free newspapers again. Its fifth or sixth page brought more news about the parachutist whose death I'd read about two days earlier. It turned out that the police had been quite right to be suspicious: an examination of the dead man's gear had unearthed evidence of tampering. The rig, or harness, he'd had strapped onto his back contained two parachutes—three if you counted the small, handkerchief-sized "drogue" that, once deployed, is meant to suck the main chute from the rig— and it had transpired that the cords attaching each of these to one another, to the rig and, ultimately, to him had been deliberately severed. The severing had been carried out with expertise and cunning; all the chutes had been repacked correctly afterwards, so that no outward sign of any interference would be visible. The deed could only have been done by an insider: someone connected to the airfield and the club, who knew the rigmarole of parachute-assembly, the protocol of jumping and jump-preparation—packing, storage, safety-checking and so forth; in short, by another parachutist. It was now a murder story. Arriving home, I drunk-phoned Madison, who didn't answer; then I passed out on my sofa.

4.

4.1 On Lévi-Strauss. He was my hero. He would roam around the world—twice: first slowly, physically, by boat and train and donkey; then all over again on fast-track as, writing his findings up, he zapped from continent to continent, culture to culture, travelling through worm-holes of association till he'd remade the entire globe into a collage of recurring colours, smells and patterns. Patterns especially: the painted patterning on tribesmen's bodies; the layout, concentric or congruent or concyclic, of village huts; the symmetry or asymmetry of caste systems, their transgenerational rhythms of exogamy and endogamy—he saw all these as co-related, parts of larger systems lying behind not just a single tribe but also the larger one of all humanity. If we had some kind of grid that we could lay across it all, he reasoned, we could establish a grand pattern of equivalences. Describing sunsets, he saw spun webs of lit-up vapour, a whole architecture of reflective strands that both revealed and hid the source that lay behind them; even landscape seemed to him to withhold, in its layers and strata, some kind of infrastructural master-meaning of which any one layer was a partial, distorted transposition. This stuff bewitched me.

Master-meaning! Concealed revealment! I spent my twenties wanting to be Lévi-Strauss—which is ironic, since he spent most of his life wanting to be somebody or something else: a philosopher, say, or novelist, or poet.

4.2 Also ironic: the very first brief I was given when I started working at the Company. I was, Tapio informed me, to compile a dossier on jeans. The client was Levi's—or, to give the company its full name, Levi Strauss. A little research unearthed more than just coincidence behind the nomenclatural overlap: the jean-maker, like the anthropologist, had been an Ashkenazi Jew; both, leaving Europe under vague or not-so-vague threat, had turned to the Americas, and built their fame on what they did there. Levi-no-hyphen-Strauss was German; but the fabric he sold came, like Lévi-Strauss, from France— from Nîmes, down in the South. *Serge de Nîmes:* denim. Nîmes serge has unique fading and dyeing properties. I spent my first three weeks of gainful employment interviewing teenagers, mid-life-crisis-riven men and garment workers; assessing the subtle code-spectrum of turn-ups, buttons, zippers, creases; generally breaking down how jeans, and Levi Strauss ones in particular, connoted. I got really into creases. Jeans crease in all kinds of interesting ways: honeycomb, whisker, train-track, stack . . . I catalogued no fewer than seventeen different crease-types, each of which has slightly different innuendos. To frame these—that is, to provide a framework for explaining to the client what these crease-types truly and profoundly *meant*—I stole a concept from the French philosopher Deleuze: for him *le pli,* or fold, describes the way we swallow the exterior world, invert it and then flip it back outwards again, and, in so doing, form our own identity. I took out all the revolutionary shit (Deleuze was a leftie); and I didn't credit Deleuze, either. Big retail companies don't want to hear about such characters. I did the same thing with another French philosopher, Badiou: I recycled his notion of a *rip,* a sudden temporal rupture, and applied it, naturally, to tears worn in jeans, which I presented as the birth-scars of their wearer's singularity, testaments to the individual's break with general history, to the successful institution of a personal time. I dropped the radical baggage from that, too (Badiou is virtually Maoist). This pretty much set up the protocol or MO I'd deploy in my work for the Company from then on in: feeding vanguard theory, almost always from the left side of the spectrum, back into the corporate machine. The machine could swallow everything, incorporate it seamlessly, like a giant loom that reweaves all fabric, no matter how recalcitrant and jarring its raw form, into what my hero would have called a master-pattern—or, if not that, then maybe just the pattern of the master.

4.3 *Le pli.* While my supposed business, my "official" function, as a corporate ethnographer, was to garner meaning from all types of situation—to extract it, like a physicist distilling some pure, unadulterated essence out of common-mongrel compounds, or a miner drawing gold ore from deep within the earth's bowels—I sometimes allowed myself to think that, in fact, things were precisely the other way round: that my job was to put meaning *in* the world, not take it from it. Divining, for the benefit of a breakfast-cereal manufacturer, the social or symbolic role of breakfast (what fasting represents, the significance of breaking it); establishing for them some of the primary axes shaping the way in which the practice of living is, or might be, carried out; and watching the manufacturer then feed that information back into their product and its packaging as they upgraded and refined these, I understood the end-result to be not simply better-tasting cereal or bigger profits for the manufacturer, but rather *meaning,* amplified and sharpened, for the millions of risers lifting cereal boxes over breakfast tables, tipping out and ingesting their contents. Helping a city council who were thinking of creating parks and plazas but had yet to understand the ethnographic logic driving such an act; laying out for them the history of public (as opposed to private) space, making them grasp what these zones fundamentally embody, what's at play in them from a political and structural and sacred point of view; and doing this in such a way that this whole history is then injected back into the squares, sports-fields and playgrounds millions of citizens will then inhabit—same thing. Down in my office, stirred and lulled by ventilation, I would picture myself as some kind of nocturnal worker, like those men who go out and repair the roads, or check the points and switches on the railway tracks, or carry out a range of covert tasks that go unnoticed by the populace-at-large, but on which the latter's well-being, even survival, is dependent. While the city sleeps, bakers are baking bread in night-kitchens, milkmen are loading crates onto their floats; and river-men are dredging riverbeds or checking water-levels, while other men in buildings with nondescript exteriors track storm surges and spring- and neap-tides on their screens, and activate the flood defences when this becomes necessary. When the populace-at-large wakes up, they just see the milk there on their doorstep, and the fresh bread in the shop down the street, and the street itself still there, unflooded, un-tsunamied from existence; and they take it all for granted, where in fact these men have *put* the milk and bread there, and have even, in deploying the flood defences, *put* the city there as well, put it *back* there every time they deploy them. That's what I was doing, too, I told myself. The world functioned, each day, because I'd put meaning back into it the day before. You didn't notice that I put it there *because* it was there; but if I'd stopped, you'd soon have known it.

4.4 I compiled a lot of dossiers. They weren't always for clients. The Company gave me *carte blanche* to follow my own nose when not working on a specific brief. I went to conferences, read (and, occasionally, wrote) articles, kept my finger on the soft pulse of the media—and compiled dossiers. I had a dossier on Japanese game-avatars, and another one on newspaper obituaries; a dossier on post-match interviews with sportsmen and their managers; a dossier on alleged alien sightings and one on shark attacks; dossiers on tattoos, "personalization" trends for hand-held gadgets, the rhetoric and diction of scam emails. These dossiers sprang up spontaneously, serendipitously, whimsically. A situation, a recurring meme would catch my eye, pique my fancy, and I'd start investigating it: following its spore, seeing where it led, collecting instances of its occurrence, assembling an inventory of all its guises and mutations; like a detective keeping a file on a quarry that's both colourful and slippery, elusive—a cat-burglar, say, or quick-change-artist con-man.

4.5 When I write "dossier," this might imply some kind of tidy, reasoned set of entries, each held in its own box-file. But the process was much less orderly: my dossiers largely consisted of scraps of paper stuck around my walls, with lines connecting them and annotations, legible only to me, scrawled at their margins. Each one would stay up for a while, then be replaced by the next one. As the scraps of paper came down, I would stuff them, usually unsorted, into large portfolios. Only the ones for clients ended up as neat, legible documents—although whether the personal whimsy-dossiers were actually so separate from the client-ones is another question. Who's to say what is, or might turn out to be, related to what else? Occasionally, a whimsy-dossier would suddenly and without warning overlap with a client-one, or with a previous whimsy- or client-one, or several of both, in quite unexpected and surprising ways, parities and conjunctions appearing between contexts that, on the surface of things, seemed to have nothing in common. When this happened, I'd feel a sudden pang, a bristling in the back of my neck: the stirring, the re-animation, of a fantasy that, like in hard-boiled novels and *noir* movies, *all* the various files would one day turn out to have been related all along, their sudden merging leading me to crack the case. What was "the case"? I didn't know—but that was the whole point: the answer to that would become clear once all the dossiers hove into alignment.

4.6 In my office, waiting for Peyman to come back to London, I began a dossier on oil spills. The oil spill that had started while I'd been in Turin was still making the news headlines, but I didn't confine myself to that one: I read about all kinds of oil spill, going right back to before the First World War. An anthropologist's not interested in singularities, but in generics. Oil spills are perfectly generic: there's always one happening, or one that's recently transpired, or, it can be said with confidence, one that's on the verge of happening. I printed off tables of data, statistics about frequencies of oil spills, their clustering by region, year and company; images of tankers trailing long, black tails; of birds coated in oil; of people in white suits pushing brooms over vinyl-coated beaches. I looped on a spare laptop a video-clip that Daniel found me: it showed a close-up sequence of a few feet of sea-bed across which oil was creeping, carpeting the floor as it coagulated. The film had been captured by a hand-held underwater camera. You could see the diver's other hand, his free one, reaching down into the shot, its white-gloved fingers feeling their way along this new-laid carpet or linoleum flooring's edge until, finding a bump or buckle that allowed for entry, the hand slid under and pulled a section of it up. The oil, still unguent, stretched as it rose. Threads, strands and filigrees appeared, thinning as they lengthened before thickening and folding in on themselves as they were gathered back by the black, undulating mass. Every time I re-watched this last piece of footage, I sensed, or thought I sensed, a smell: the sweet, familiar scent of homemade toffee at the point—that magical instant—of caramelization. That's what these pictures, even through the airless medium of water and the odourless relays of fibre-optic cable, through the mangling of digital compression, the delays, decays and abstractions brought about by storage and conversion, managed to transmit to me.

4.7 As I watched this sequence over and over again (it was only about forty seconds long), other recognizable scenes began exuding from it. The diver's gesture, for example— reaching down and pulling up the solidifying oil—was familiar as well: it was the gesture of a priest raising the holy water in his fingers, or a jeweler displaying a valuable necklace, or a zoologist handling a sleek, endangered snake. The diver, naturally, would have held the camera right beside his face, or perhaps in front of it, pressed up against his mask. This point of view produced another strange, confectionary-oriented pang of recognition; each time I watched, I felt my own face and the diver's run together. I knew the look on his because it was the look on mine—not only then, watching the clip, but also once when, on a childhood holiday to San Francisco many years ago, I'd stood rooted to the pavement in front of a candy-store window in which taffy was being pulled, transfixed by the contortions of the huge, unmanageable lump (what child could eat all *that*?) as the machine's arms plied it, its endless metamorphoses in which, despite the regular, repeating movements that stretched and folded, stretched and slapped the taffy through the same shapes over and over again, I knew, even then, that no part of it, no molecule, would ever occupy the same spot in the overall formation twice.

4.8 Eventually, after days spent immersed in this material, I received a call from Tapio upstairs. Peyman's on his way back, his robot-voice intoned. Come and see him on Friday. Okay, I said. How's the Great Report coming along? he asked before he hung up. Oh, you know, I answered: it's finding its form. Five minutes after he'd called, Petr called too. Hey, he said: you know that goiter they were going to take out? Yes, I replied. Well, he told me, they did; and then they cut it up to look at it, and it was cancerous. Shit, I said. Yes, he said. Good thing they took it out, I said. No, U., he said, the goiter's just an indicator: I've got thyroid cancer. Shit, I said again. Yes, he repeated—but it's not that bad. How come? I asked. Because, he said, as cancers go, thyroid is a pretty lowly one: a lickspittle of cancers, a cadet. It's almost never fatal. What do you have to do? I asked. I have to drink a bunch of iodine, he said. It soaks up all the bad cells and destroys them. It will make me radioactive. I'll be going round town oozing rays and isotopes, like a plutonium rod. Far out, I said. Yes, he said: I'll be able to look straight through girls' clothes and see what colour underwear they've got on. Really? I asked. Of course not, he said. But I will ooze rays. Far out, I said again; I didn't know what else to say. Yeah, he repeated: far out.

4.9 On my way home that evening, I opened the free newspaper again, and found a photo of the airfield where the recently killed parachutist's club was based. The photo showed a hangar and a runway cordoned off by police tape, with an officer standing in front of this to ensure that visitors and press stayed out. Something struck me as not quite right about the image. The officer was oddly poised—slightly unbalanced, as though starting to move off in such-and-such a direction but not yet fully launched into his walk. It wasn't this that was wrong, though: it was the choice of restricted area itself. If a person had been shot or stabbed within the airfield's boundary, it would have made sense for there to be a cordon round it; but this man had died on landing in a field some distance away. Presumably that field was cordoned off as well. But even that location didn't accurately represent the one at which the crime had actually taken place: just where its consequences had played out, left their imprint. The crime itself, the moment of its actually-happening, would have occurred when, just after he threw his drogue out, as he awaited the familiar jolt and the ensuing drag, the reassuring easing of his downward plummet brought on by the opening of the parachute itself, the victim realized that these things hadn't occurred, that he was still in freefall. The happening-moment would have taken place a second time after he'd pulled his ripcord and again felt no consoling bite, met with no purchase on the air around him; and a third when he'd attempted to deploy his reserve chute, equally fruitlessly. Did that mean there'd been three crimes instead of one? Perhaps. As I held the page above my knees, sat on a tube train shuttling through a tunnel, the question of the murder's true location resolved itself for me: I realized that the crime scene, properly speaking, was the sky. Or, to flip this one back out as well: the sky was a crime scene.

5.

5.1 On the Company. No: on companies; on companies and crowds; whatever. In the fifties and sixties, people like me started conducting studies of corporations, presenting their findings back to the academy, for consecration as pure, unconditional knowledge. But, sometime in the seventies or eighties, all that changed: now anthropologists found themselves working *for* the corporation, not *on* it. So it was with me. It was the Company itself within whose remit I was operating. To whom did I report? The Company. Nonetheless, it was hard not to analyze the Company's own make-up along anthropological lines. In fact, it was impossible. Forget family, or ethnic and religious groupings: corporations have supplanted all these as the primary structure of the modern tribe. My use of the word *tribe* here isn't fanciful; it's *modern* that's the dubious term. The logic underlying the corporation is completely primitive. The corporation has its gods, its fetishes, its high priests and its outcasts (Madison was right about that part—just wrong in thinking this makes it exotic). It has its rituals, beliefs and superstitions, its pools of homespun expertise and craft and, conversely, its Unknowns or Unspokens. Peyman understood this. When he first hired me he told me that the Company needed an anthropologist because its entire field of operations lay in analyzing groups, picking apart their operations and reporting back on this, while at the same time both appreciating and refining its own status as a group, *de facto* subject to the same ongoing (and productive) scrutiny. At base, it's all already anthropology, he said.

5.2 Peyman said lots of things. That's what he did: put ideas out, put them in circulation. He did this via publications, websites, talks at conferences; via the quasi-governmental think tanks he was constantly invited to head up, or the interviews he'd give in the trade press. His ideas took the form of aphorisms: *Location is irrelevant: what matters is not where something is, but rather where it leads . . . What are objects? Bundles of relations . . .* Each of these nuggets was instantly memorable, eminently quotable. On urbanism: *A city has no "character"; it is a schizoid headspace, filled with the cacophony of contradiction.* On design: *The end point to which it strives is a state in which the world is one hundred percent synthetic, made by man, for man, according to his desires . . .* These aphorisms were his currency; he traded in them, converting them, via the Company, into tangible undertakings that had measurable outcomes, which in turn helped spawn more concepts and more aphorisms, always at a profit. The concepts were all generated in-house and collectively: that's how his outfit worked. We'd come at briefs, and at the big ones in particular, from several angles, bringing all our intellectual disciplines to bear on them—the Company had people who'd trained as economists, philosophers, mathematicians, architects and who knows what else on its books—and, slapping the pertinent offerings of each of these down on the collective table (or up on the collective sheet of glass), formulate new concepts that Peyman, as the Company's public face and poster-boy, would then launch into circulation. Seeing these in print, observing them being cited, appropriated, sampled, cross-bred, both by others and by Peyman himself, was like encountering an amalgam of our own minds, our own thoughts, returning to us on a feedback loop. Without Peyman, though, without the general—and generative—mechanism he had set in place and over which he constantly presided, we would never have come up with these thoughts in the first place: they were quite beyond us.

5.3 Thus Peyman, for us, was everything and nothing. Everything because he connected us, both individually and severally, our scattered, half-formed notions and intuitions, fields of research which would otherwise have lain fallow, found no bite and purchase on the present moment—he connected all these to a world of action and event, a world in which stuff might actually *happen;* connected us, that is, to our own age. And not just us: it worked the same way for the Company's clients. That's what they were buying into: connection and connectedness—to ideas, expertise, the universe of consequence, the age. It sometimes seemed as though the very concept of "the age" wouldn't have been fully thinkable without Peyman; seemed that he invented, re-invented it with every passing utterance, or simply (with the overlay of continents and times and cultures stored up in his very genes, his mixed Persian, South American and European ancestry) by existing. He connected the age to itself, and, in so doing, called it into being. And, at the same time, he was nothing. Why? Because, in playing this role, he underwent a kind of reverse camouflage (some anthropologists do speak of such a thing). The concepts he helped generate and put in circulation were so perfectly tailored *to* the age on whose high seas they floated, their contours so perfectly aligned with those of the reality from which they were drawn and onto which they constantly remapped themselves, that you'd find yourself coming across some new phenomenon, some trend—in architecture or town planning or brand strategy or social policy, in Europe, the States, India, it didn't matter what or where—and saying: *Oh, Peyman came up with a term for this;* or: *That's a Peyman thing.* You'd find yourself saying this several times a week—that is, seeing tendencies Peyman had named or invented, Peymanic paradigms and inclinations, movements and precipitations, everywhere, till he appeared in everything; which is the same as disappearing.

5.4 He disappeared in a quite literal sense for us, his Company underlings. I mean that he was hardly ever actually, in an in-the-flesh way, *there:* on almost any given day he'd be off in Oslo, or São Paulo, or Mumbai, meeting with high-powered

clients, advising presidents and mayors, or just generally helping draw up blueprints for the future of the world. Sometimes
I almost doubted his existence. Not literally, of course: I knew
that the dusty-skinned man bearing Peyman's name was Peyman. But I wondered sometimes whether, like in that Hitch-
cock movie *North by Northwest,* whose lead character finds
himself inhabiting a role that's been established elsewhere and
already, Peyman didn't function as some kind of construct, a
convenient front. For whom? I don't know. What Machia-
vellian cabal, what shady interest group, what nefarious—if
inspired—alliance of the influential and manipulative, with
what tools and channels at their beck and call, could maintain this type of illusion? In reality, no such cabal was needed.
Gods, for many tribes, are self-sustaining, and perpetuate
their operation without ranks of priests pulling the witch-hut's
levers and ventriloquising for the carved idols. Like a god, Peyman withdrew, secluded himself from us, took up spectral res-
idence within some sacred recess full of ministers and moguls
over whom *he* held sway, not the other way around. I'd imagine
him consorting with them all, surrounded by them like a sultan
by his harem. But, of course, for them as well, he was secluded;
from them, too, withdrawn. He, after all, would drop into their
offices and ministries, then jet back out again. They probably
envisioned him consorting with us back in his (to their minds)
mystical headquarters—and (who knows?) maybe also wondered, in their more reflective moments, whether he wasn't
some kind of collective fantasy, a self-sustaining deity whose
nature they didn't really understand but in whom they still had

to *believe,* because, well, if not him, then . . . what? I took some solace in the thought of them picturing us—me—haremed up with him, bathed in his connective radiance constantly, day after day. Although, of course, I wasn't: I was sat down in a basement, listening to ventilation.

5.5 The Company's logo was a giant, crumbling tower. It was Babel, of course, the old biblical parable. It embodied one of Peyman's signature concepts. Babel's tower, he'd say, is usually taken to be a symbol of man's hubris. But the myth, he'd carry on, has been misunderstood. What actually matters isn't the attempt to reach the heavens, or to speak God's language. No: what matters is what's left when that attempt has failed. This ruinous edifice (he'd say), which serves as a glaring reminder that its would-be occupants are scattered about the earth, spread horizontally rather than vertically, babbling away in all these different tongues—this tower becomes of interest only once it has flunked its allotted task. Its ruination is the precondition for all subsequent exchange, all cultural activity. And, on top of that, despite its own demise, the tower remains: you see it there in all the paintings—ruined, but still rising with its arches and its buttresses, its jagged turrets and its rusty scaffolding. What's valuable about it is its uselessness. Its uselessness sets it to work: as symbol, cipher, spur to the imagination, to productiveness. The first move for any strategy of cultural production, he'd say, must be to liberate things—objects, situations, systems—into uselessness. I read this for the first time, long before I worked for him, in *Creative Review;* then later, with slight variations, in *Design Monthly, Contemporary Business Journal* and *Icon.*

5.6 Another concept that he put about a lot, that was much quoted: narrative. If I had, he'd say, to sum up, in a word, what we (the Company, that is) essentially do, I'd choose not *consultancy* or *design* or *urban planning*, but *fiction*. Fiction? asks the interviewer (this one comes from *Consulting Today*—but he says the same thing in his *Urban Futures* profile; and in the RIBA transcripts). Fiction, Peyman repeats. The city and the state are fictional conditions; a business is a fictional entity. Even if it's real, it's still a construct. Lots of the Company's projects have been fictions that became real. For example? asks the interviewer. For example, Peyman answers, the EU commissioned us to imagine what a concrete affirmation of a European commonality might look like—purely speculatively, you understand. So we designed a flag. It didn't really look much like a flag—more like a rainbow bar-code formed of strips of all the colours of the member-nations' flags. Once we'd come up with it, we Photoshopped it into a bunch of pictures: of the EC President giving a speech; finance ministers from member-states sitting round a table; even entrances to governmental buildings in a range of European capitals. We'd find a suggestive photo, then adapt it. The images caused a furore. No one stopped to ask if they were real. The conservative press denounced these bar-code ensigns, called them illegitimate; progressives, though, adopted them, so real ones started springing up. Thus the facts, in this case, followed from the fiction. Fiction was what engendered them and held them in formation. We should view all propositions and all projects this way.

5.7 His most famous riff, perhaps, was about knowledge. Not knowledge *of* anything in particular; just knowledge in and of itself. Who was the last person, he would ask, to enjoy a full command of the intellectual activity of their day? The last *individual*, I mean? It was, he'd answer, Leibniz. He was on top of it all: physics and chemistry, geology, philosophy, maths, engineering, medicine, theology, aesthetics. Politics too. I mean, the guy was *on* it. Like some universal joint in the giant Rubik's Cube of culture, he could bring it all together, make the arts and sciences dance to the same tune. He died three hundred years ago. Since Leibniz's time (Peyman would go on), the disciplines have separated out again. They're now on totally different pages: each in its own stall, shut off from all the others. Our own era, perhaps more than any other, seems to call out for a single intellect, a universal joint to bring them all together once again—seems to demand, in other words, a Leibniz. Yet there will be no Leibniz 2.0. What there *will* be is an endless set of migrations: knowledge-parcels travelling from one field to another, and mutating in the process. No one individual will conduct this operation; it will be performed collectively, with input from practitioners of a range of crafts, possessors of a range of expertise. Migration, mutation, and what I (Peyman affirmed) call "supercession": the ability of each and every practice to surpass itself, break its own boundaries, even to the point of sacrificing its own terms and tenets in the breaching; and, in the no-man's-land between its territory and the next, the blank stretches of the map, those interstitial zones where light, bending and kinking round impossible topographies, produces mirages, *fata morganas,* apparitions, spectres, to combine in new, fantastic and explosive ways. That, he'd say, is the future of knowledge.

5.8 When I went up to meet him on the fifth floor— whenever I went there, I mean—the thing that would impress itself upon me most, the thing I'd most remember afterwards, wasn't the meeting itself, but rather its peripherals: the angle of approach towards his office; the tap my heels made on the wooden boards; the reflections in the glass partition separating his room from the rest of the floor—reflections of reflections, since the whole floor had (as I mentioned earlier) these glass screens that ghost-doubled one another. The few feet just before this last partition lay within a blind spot whose occupant, or traverser, would be hidden from the rest of the floor's view—invisible, in other words, to the many people who worked in all the other glass-partitioned spaces. Each time I entered and moved through this stretch, I'd hold my right hand up beside my head and click its fingers—three times, *click-click-click.* I don't know why I did it; it was a kind of tic, made all the more enjoyable by the knowledge that only *I* would ever experience or even know about it; in the midst of all the overload and noise, a small, private act, and a small, private enclave for the act's appreciation. I did it every time I came to visit Peyman—and, each time I did, the couple of seconds it took me to do it merged with the couple of seconds it had taken me to do it last time, and the time before, and every time since I'd first done it, not to mention all the times that I would do it in the future; so I found myself transported, for those—for all those—seconds, into a kind of timelessness in which only this act and its unfolding, this now-eternal *click-click-click*ing of my right hand's fingers, did or could exist.

5.9 That Friday, when I went up to see him, he greeted me, without removing his gaze from the hand-held into which he was typing a message, with a question. As I stepped out of the blind spot back into time and his office, he asked: Have you ever been to Seattle, U.? Behind him, through the floor-to-ceiling windows, cranes, clouds, bridges, aeroplanes, the Thames all jostled for position. No, I answered. It's interesting, he said. Oh yes? I asked. How so? Well, he replied, the truly striking thing about the city is its lack of Starbucks outlets: driving around, you don't see a single one. That's strange, I said; I thought Seattle was where Starbucks came from. *Exactly,* he said; you'd think the town would turn out to just be one giant Starbucks. But instead it's all *Joe's Cappuccino Bar, Espresso Luigi, Pacific Coffee Shack* and the like. So what's the story there? I asked. What's the story indeed? he repeated.

This is exactly what I asked my driver; and do you know what he told me? Peyman looked up from his device. I shook my head. He told me, Peyman said, his gaze now drifting over to his monitor, that these *were* Starbucks: *stealth* ones. Starbucks' management, their strategists, understand that no one actually wants to buy coffee from Starbucks; they do it for convenience, heads hung low with shame. People crave authenticity, locality and (here his speech slowed down a little, since he'd started typing again) . . . origin—everything that Starbucks, as a global chain, represents the polar opposite of. So the strategists (he went on) create these "local" figures—Joe, Luigi and the like—and launch a handful of outlets for each, not too near to one another, and see how they fare: real-world R&D. If one takes off, they'll roll it out nationwide, and across Europe, Asia and the rest—and everyone will flock to it, because it isn't Starbucks. Isn't that brilliant? he asked. Yes, I replied; I guess it is.

5.10 He proceeded to brief me on the Project; the Company's role in this; my own within that. There'd be a meeting with the Minister in a few weeks' time; he wanted me to come; he wanted me to go to Paris; he wanted me to continue following my own lines (or sidelines) of intuitive enquiry, and report back intermittently on these, as always; there was other stuff. I'm being quite vague, in part because I'm obliged to be; but in part because he was quite vague as well. He'd always been that way: his currency also comprised, as its reserve, a kind of systematic vagueness. *Some spaces of ignorance do not need* *to be filled in*—that was another of his aphorisms. His whole knack, the USP on which he'd built his business, was for managing uncertainties, for somehow joining isolated dots into a constellation-pattern people could just—*just*—recognize, and be seduced by. As I listened to him talk about Koob-Sassen, it all made sense, even if it didn't. Even the fact that it didn't quite make sense made sense, while he was talking.

5.II Later that evening, I saw Madison again. Again we had sex. Afterwards, lying in bed, I found my mind drifting, once more, among images of oil. I moved through dark and ponderous swells, black-cresting waves and fleck-spattered shingles, before settling among pools in which oil, spent and inert, lay draped over rocks and animals alike. When it covered whole rocks and whole animals, it looked like PVC, like fetish gear. The rescue and clean-up teams' protective suits looked both perverse and prophylactic at the same time. Offshore, where the waves were breaking, I could see a sluttish Aphrodite frolicking in blackened foam, her face adorned with the look that readers' wives and models have in dirty magazines.

6.

6.1 The following week, I organized a meeting with a bunch of civil servants who were working on Koob-Sassen. The idea was that they'd sit in a room and discuss their sense of what the Project entailed, or, more subtly, implied. We had, in the Company's offices, a room purpose-built for such discussions. It had loungers, sofas, armchairs, even beanbags—all chosen to induce as relaxed and casual an atmosphere as possible, so that the discussion's participants could just chew the fat while we watched them through a two-way mirror that formed one of the room's walls. It never worked that way, of course: people always knew that they were being watched, assessed, recorded. It's a well-known problem for the anthropologist, first noted by a man named Landsberger: the tribe under observation are aware they're being observed, and alter their behaviour in view of this fact, often acting out versions of themselves which they think conform to the ethnographer's own conceptions of them. The technical term for this phenomenon is the Hawthorne effect; but in college we always called it the Cat-in-a-Box Paradox. Our nickname owed its title to the famous hypothesis

devised by Erwin Schrödinger, to illustrate the logical consequences of Einstein's discoveries about the weird behaviour of
atoms (we were, in fact, slightly confusing two separate scientific
theorems—the Hawthorne effect doesn't actually have much
to do with Schrödinger's hypothesis; but, not being quantum
physicists, we didn't know or care). Were you (Schrödinger
proposed) to seal a cat inside a box in which a vial of gaseous
poison—cyanide, say—would either break, thereby killing the
cat, or remain intact, thereby leaving it unharmed, depending
on which of two apertures an atom chose to jump through—
well, the atom would only choose to *have jumped* through one
hole or the other at the moment when the scientist opened up
the box to see which it had *already* jumped through. In other
words, the cat would be neither alive nor dead, or rather, *both*
alive *and* dead, until the scientist, *post hoc,* peered in to ascertain its live- or deadness.

6.2 Thus it was, after a manner, with the subjects I'd observe
through the fake mirror. These civil servants knew without
being told what was expected of them—not by me, nor even
by their bosses, their immediate superiors to whom they could
attribute a name and face and rank, but rather by some larger
and much vaguer host of assessors, overviewers, judges, lurking on the far side of some other two-way mirror much, much
larger, if less obvious, than this one—and were shaping their
contributions accordingly. They kept using the word "excite-

ment" (one hundred and eighty-two occurrences over three hours); also "challenge" (one hundred and four); "opportunity" (eighty-nine); "transformation" (seventy-eight); and, as an upscale variant on this last word, "re-configuration" (sixty-three). They reclined in their loungers, stretched their legs out from their beanbags, tried to exude nonchalance and calm—but to me they transmitted tenseness and unease, like anxious cats.

6.3 The way iodine works, said Petr when we met later that week in the same pub as last time—what it does, is it *recognizes* thyroid cancer-cells and zaps them. Say each cancer-cell was like a coin—a certain type, from a specific period, with an exact denomination—well, iodine is trained to spot this coin and melt it back down, take it out of circulation. That sounds pretty straight-forward, I said. You'll be cured, then. Ah, he replied: in principle it sounds straight-forward. But in practice it turns out to be a little harder than I thought. He paused. How do you mean? I asked. Well, he said, say one of these coins is degraded, or a little different, through some quirk of the mint—the way a machine-part was lying the day that it was pressed, a piece of grit that found its way into the mix, a hundred other permutation-causing factors we could mention: then the iodine can't recognize it, since these variations haven't been included in its recognition-software. So the coin, the cancer-cell, not only stays in circulation; it sets up its own mint and prints new copies of itself, each one corrupt, unrecognizable as well; and then these introduce new variations and new mint-quirks of their own, until the iodine has no idea what it's even supposed to be looking for, throws its hands up, mutters *Fuck this!* and heads off home. It's a systems problem, Petr said. If we had a better database, then I'd be out of danger.

6.4 One afternoon, while sorting through the transcript of the civil-servant dialogues down in the basement, I poked my head into Daniel's office again. This time I found him staring at footage that showed hundreds of legs gliding through city streets. I say "gliding" because that's what they were doing, rather than (say) walking or running. The legs, I realized after a few seconds, belonged to roller-bladers: lots of roller-bladers, skating past the camera—which itself, since it was moving, was (presumably) being held by somebody also on roller-blades. How's the Great Report coming along? Daniel asked. Oh, you know, I said: it's coming along slowly; still finding its shape. Look at the way they move, said Daniel, without turning his head towards me. I looked: the bladers' heads all angled forwards, focused on a spot beyond the picture's frame, some point on which they were advancing. It wasn't a race: there was no urgency to their pace. More like a Friday-evening meet-up (it was dark; the streets were lit), with most people just ambling forwards, or sliding from one side of the moving column to the other, or letting the column's body flow ahead of them a little as they waited for an acquaintance to catch up, or checked their phone for messages, or fiddled with the music they had plugged into their ears.

6.5 I shot it in Paris, Daniel said, still facing away from me towards the wall. I'm going there next week, I told him. It's an MSP, he said, ignoring me. What's that? I asked. *Manifestation sans Plainte,* he answered. That's the legal term for it, as set out in the license granted by the Paris *mairie:* a Demonstration With No Complaint. Oh, I said; and we watched the footage in silence for a little longer. The roller-bladers kept on gliding by. They didn't have to make much of an effort to progress, since the street's surface was quite smooth. This gave them all a kind of languid look. Paris, Daniel explained when I commented on the pavement's texture, has the smoothest street surface of any major European city. It's because of sixty-eight, he said, the general uprisings, when revolutionaries pulled up all the cobblestones to throw them at the cops. They even had a slogan stirring them to do this: *Underneath the paving stones, the beach!* After that, he explained, the authorities replaced the paving stones with tarmac—which had the unforeseen effect of turning the city into a paradise for roller-bladers.

6.6 I kept thinking about the dead parachutist. The circumstances of the incident recalled a chapter from my own childhood. I can pinpoint, with complete precision, the episode that set me on my career path: it occurred when, at the age of seven, I happened to watch, one rainy Sunday afternoon, a documentary—an old one, from the early sixties—about South Pacific islanders. These people, Vanuatans, engaged once a year in a peculiar ritual: the men would climb a high and rickety-looking wooden tower and, goaded on by their womenfolk, who chanted songs of exhortation, leap from the top of this, head first. They wore vines round their ankles, cut to such a length that they would tauten just before the men's torsos crashed into the earth below. After watching the documentary, I'd climb up my younger sisters' bunk-bed and, fastening T-shirts and pyjamas round my ankles and the bedpost, leap repeatedly, head first, towards the carpet. If a Vanuatan hesitated or refused a dive, his womenfolk would whip themselves with thorns and nettles, to shame him into action; I made my sisters whip themselves with flannels. I performed the ritual for several days, until a dislocated shoulder and my parents' veto brought an end to it—but by then, the documentary had done its work. From that time onwards, when people asked me what I wanted to be when I grew up, I'd tell them: *anthropologist.*

6.7 So, with this parachutist: I'd already, as I mentioned, figured out the crime's location (the sky). The question remained, though, of timing. In other words: at what precise *point* in time had he actually been murdered? When the equipment had been sabotaged? If he'd survived the fall—been greeted by a sudden upgust of ground-wind, say, or landed in soft, deep snow, or in the branches of a fir-tree that, pliant and supple, had broken his fall incrementally as he tumbled through them, each layer shaving a little more velocity away until the last layer rolled him gently onto needle-covered earth—if any of these miracles (of which popular lore is, after all, quite full) had taken place, the act of sabotage wouldn't have constituted murder. Yet, as at least one article I read stated, the man's death was, in this instance—in this country devoid of tall pine trees, this terrain quite unamenable to upgusts, this snow-less season—a foregone conclusion from the moment the cords had been cut. Thus, although he hadn't actually been killed until the moment of his impact, to all intents and purposes, he had. For the last hours—days, perhaps—of his life, he had (this is how Schrödinger would formulate it) *been* murdered without *realizing* it. I tried to picture him walking around in that state: already effectively dead, his body and his consciousness, his experiences, and, beyond these, his experience of his experiences—his awareness of himself, his whole reality—mere side effects of a technical delay, a pause, an interval; an interval comparable, perhaps, to the ones you get down phone-lines when you speak long distance or on Skype: just the hiatus created by the passage of a command down a chain, the sequence of its parts; the interim between an action and its motion, like those paralytic lags that come in hideous dreams.

6.8 The Great Report: this needs explaining. It was Peyman's idea. When he first hired me, as he shook my hand to welcome me onboard, he fixed me with his gaze and said: U., write the Great Report. The Great Report? I asked, my hand still clenched in his; what's that? The Document, he said; the Book. The First and Last Word on our age. Over and above all the other work you'll do here at the Company, that's what I'm *really* hiring you to come up with. It's what you anthropologists are for, right? Could you elaborate? I asked. Well, he replied, finally letting my hand go so that he could gesticulate with his; you don your khakis, schlep off to some jungle, hang out with the natives, fish and hunt with them, shiver from their fevers, drink strange brew fermented in their virgins' mouths, and all the rest; then, after about a year, they lug your bales and cases down to the small jetty that connects their tiny world to the big one that they kind of know exists, but only as an abstract concept, like adultery for children; and, waving with big, gap-toothed smiles, they send you back to your study—where, khakis swapped for cotton shirt and tie, saliva-liquor for the Twinings, tisane or iced Scotch your housekeeper purveys you on a tray, you write the book: that's what I mean, he said. Not just *a* book: *the* fucking *Book*. You write the Book on them. Sum their tribe up. Speak its secret name.

6.9 His phone rang at this point. He took the call, and spoke in German (fluent) for five minutes. When he'd finished, he looked up at me and asked me if I saw what he was driving at. I do, I told him. But, I started—then I faltered. But what? he asked. Your version, I said . . . vision, I mean, depiction—

then, striking upon the right word—*characterization*, of the anthropologist . . . What of it? he asked. Well, I said, it might have been an accurate one a century ago. But now there are no natives—or *we*'re the natives. I mean . . . I know, I know all that stuff, he said, cutting me off. I've read your clubbing-tome: kaleidoscopes; personae; passing out in toilets; it's all good. And it's exactly the situation you describe, he carried on, that makes *our* era's Great Report all the more necessary. Shifting tectonics, new islands and continents forming: we need a brand-new navigation manual. But also, I tried to tell him, now there is no study, with its housekeeper and Scotch and tisane. I mean, there are universities . . . Forget universities! he snorted, interrupting me again. These are irrelevant; they've become businesses—and not even good ones. *Real* businesses, though, he said, his hand describing in the air above his desk a circle that encompassed the whole building: these are the forge, the foundry where true knowledge is being smelted, cast and hammered out. You're right, U.: there is no tranquil study. But the Great Report won't be composed in a study; it will come out of the jungle, breaking cover like some colourful, fantastic beast, a species never seen before, a brand-new genus, flashing, sparkling—*fulgurating*—high above the tree-line, there for all to see. I want it to come out of the Company. We're the noblest savages of all. We're sitting with our war-paint at the spot where all the rivers churn and flow together. The Company, he repeated, his voice growing louder with excitement, is the place for it to come from; you, U., are the one to write it.

He carried on looking straight at me, into me. He was smiling, but the way his dark eyes fixed me made it clear that, smile or no smile, he was deadly serious. What I want you to do, he said, is *name* what's taking place right now. To name it? I repeated; like the princess does with Rumpelstiltskin in the fairytale? Yes, he said: exactly. What do you want this Great Report to look like? I asked. What form should it take? To whom should it be addressed? These are secondary questions, he said. I leave it to you to work them out. It will find its shape.

6.10 Had it, when these events (*q.v.*) took place, found its shape? It was finding it—*finding* it in the same way we might say that we're *looking* for an object rather than that it's lost or non-existent. Shapes were happening inside my thought; or, rather, shap*ings*, a preliminary set of shifts and swirls, coherences and separations of the type that, in their overall movement, seem to promise shape and structure somewhere further down the line. Frames, contexts, modes, tones, formats would suggest themselves—pipe up, step forwards, as though volunteering for a task—then, no sooner than they'd made their willingness and presence known to me, fall silent again, slink back into the crowd and disappear. But these spectral presences, and the promise they (like all ghosts) carried that they might return, helped add momentum to all my enquiries, each of my dossiers, no matter how isolated and idiosyncratic their subject-matter seemed: after all, might this or that one not turn out, in addition to whatever other function it performed, to be the spur to set the Great Report, by happy accident, agalloping? Although I had done nothing concrete to begin the thing, simply being under starter's orders in this way lent a background radiance, a promise of significance, to everything I did. At the same time, it sent my general levels of anxiety, already high, still higher.

6.11 Back in my basement, in between various new tasks demanded of me by the Koob-Sassen Project—and against the constant, second-level mental puzzling laid down for me since my first day at the Company by this separate, all-important charge, this Great Report—I started a file on parachutists. Dead ones: ones whose parachutes had failed to open. It's surprising how many times the story, or a variant on it, pops up: like oil spills, it's generic. Even when I'd first read, on the tube, the initial three-line article about the episode, I'd had a sense of déjà-vu, a sense of having read this article, or one very like it, at least once before. *Oh, a dead parachutist: one of those.* Everyone can recognize and understand that situation. Before I'd ever heard of Vanuatans, the first joke I learnt to tell as a child was about a classified ad for a used parachute, "no strings attached." To the anthropologist, as I explained before, it's generic episodes and phenomena that stand out as significant, not singular ones. To the anthropologist, there's no such thing as a singular episode, a singular phenomenon—only a set of variations on generic ones; the more generic, therefore, the more pure, the closer to an unvariegated or unscrambled archetype. The parachutist story, in the stark, predictable simplicity of the circumstance that it presented, in the boldness of its second-handness, was refreshing: in its unashamed lack of originality, it was original.

6.12 The strange thing was, the more I started looking for dead parachutists, the more they started cropping up—in real time, I mean. Sure, I unearthed instances of parachutes failing to open, and suspicions being aired as to the cause, running back fifty years. There'd been a case in America where both main chute and reserve had ripped on opening, despite the odds against this happening from fabric fatigue alone being about ten million to one; and another one in Australia where a harness had quite inexplicably caught fire in mid-air; and so forth. But, in the very period during which I was compiling these cases—a period of no more than two and a half months—no less than three more stories hit the news involving parachutists slamming into the ground chuteless. They weren't in England: one took place in New Zealand; one in Poland; one in Canada. And, of course, the particulars varied—but they all involved suspected acts of sabotage; and none of the cases, over this same period, was resolved. The replication, or near-replication, of these situations started buzzers ringing all over my head—and made the case of my own parachutist, the unfortunate soul whose death had snagged my interest in the first place, all the more gripping: an originally un-original event becoming even more un-original, and hence even more fascinating.

6.13 One day, I went to Paris, and conducted the same type of staged enquiries that I'd carried out in London: a group of financial-service workers this time. There was no mirror; but I had a translator beside me, repeating phrases I'd half-understood on their first iteration softly in my ear. I left in the morning and came back in the evening. Daniel was right: the streets are all tarmaced and smooth. I hadn't noticed that before. I also noticed that the Eurostar trains have a small but niggling design fault: when they attain top speed, the vacuum created beneath their undercarriage sucks the surrounding air in and funnels this on upwards through the intermittently open toilet flaps, with the result that urine blows back in the urinator's face. I mused that, should the Company ever find itself hired by its former EU client's sworn adversaries—hired, that is, by some right-wing, Europhobic lobby group—to come up with a symbol to express *their* cause, I would propose this glitch, this blowback water-feature.

6.14 Madison phoned me while I was still on the train. When are you back? she asked. Tonight, I said. I want you here right now, she told me. Come straight to mine when you get in. I did. Lying in bed later, after we'd had sex, instead of picturing oil as I fell asleep like I had last time, my mind drifted through black streets. They were the streets of Paris—not so much the real Paris I'd just visited as an imaginary Paris formed in my head through the repetition of the fifty or so feet of it that had made up the background of Daniel's roller-blading film. These streets, as I said, were black, all stripped of cobblestones and covered in a smooth, continuous tarmac coat. This coat was unrolling as I glided forward: unrolling more and more, decking the boulevards and avenues and alleyways in soft, black oblivion. Occasionally, as I passed such-and-such a spot, I'd be made half-aware that some historical event, some revolutionary episode, had taken place just there—but even as the knowledge flashed up it was extinguished, buried beneath the tarmac. This happened over and over again: whatever acts of insurrection, of defiance, or their markers and memorials, sprung up in an attempt to catch and trip the passing gaze, these were all smoothed out, muffled, drowned. The tarmac ran on endlessly, running each street into the next as I advanced along them, heading nowhere in particular, just gliding, on and on; on either side, at the periphery of my vision, coffee-chain concessions ran together, like the tarmac, in a smooth, unbroken blur. There was nothing dramatic about this; it wasn't a disaster. No one was complaining, or even surprised: it was just the way it was. *That's just the way it is,* a voice inside my head, perhaps my own, said. I might even have said it out aloud. Madison kind of grunted in her half-sleep. Then we were both gone.

7.

7.1 The Koob-Sassen Project. I won't, as I've already stated, talk of this—and yet, during this period, everyone did, all the time. They discussed it not as people discuss things they know about, subjects whose properties and parameters are given, but rather as they try to ascertain those of a foreign object, one that is at once both present—omnipresent—and elusive: groping after its dimensions; trying, through mutual enquiry, to discern its composition, charge and limit. When, in the course of my professional activities, I asked people to provide a visual image that, for them, most represented it, I got answers varying from hovering spaceship to rabbit warren to pond lilies. I had my own, of course: I saw towers rising in the desert—splendid, ornate constructions, part modern skyscraper, part sultan's palace lifted from *Arabian Nights:* steel and glass columns segueing into vaulted cupolas and stilted arches, tiled *muqarnas,* dwindling minarets that seemed, at their cloud-laced peaks, to shed their own materiality, turn into vapour. Below them, hordes of people—thousands, tens of thousands—laboured, moving around like ants, their circuits forming patterns on the sand; patterns that, in their amalgam, coalesced into one larger, more coherent pattern, just as the meandering, bowing, divagating stretches of a river delta do when seen from high enough above. What were they doing, all these ant-like labourers? Why, they were bringing in materials, or carrying out excavated soil, or delivering instructions they themselves, perhaps, did not quite understand, nor even, fully, did the person to whom they were relaying them, so complex was the logic governing the Project as a whole—instructions, though, whose serial execution, even if full comprehension was beyond the scope of any single point in the command-chain, had the effect of moving the whole intricate scheme towards its glorious realization, at which point *all* would become clear, to everyone, and ants would see as gods.

7.2 I had this vision often; as the weeks and months progressed, the edifice within it neared completion, its plan and outline growing more apparent. There were still unfinished bits, though: gaping lacunae where the carapace gave way to reveal guttery of half-laid floors, bare wiring, strata opening onto sub- and super-strata, down and up and every which way. The distances, the heights and depths and spaces in between, were huge—it was an entire metropolis, a Tower (and here, of course, the Company's own logo wormed its way into the picture) of Babel. Peyman would always be there, in these visions: he'd be standing on the plain, perched on a balcony, or leaning against a half-completed buttress, consorting with engineers and princes, architects and sheiks and viziers, tweaking some finer point of the overall plan, or going over the logistics for the next phase, or some such activity—there in the thick of it, *connected;* and I, through my association with him, felt connected too. Even if this isn't what the Project *actually* involved, this is how it presented itself to me, as I sat down in my basement, rode the tube, or drifted off to sleep.

7.3 The meeting with the Minister took place. It's odd to spend time in the company of somebody with power—I mean real, executive power: to hang out with a powerful person. You would imagine they exude this power at every turn, with each one of their gestures; that their very bodies sweat the stuff, wafting its odour at you through expensive clothes. But in fact, the thing most noticeable about this Minister was her lack of powerful aura. She seemed very normal. She wasn't physically striking in any way: neither particularly tall nor particularly short; neither fat nor thin; neither attractive nor ugly. Her accent bore no traces of excessive privilege, nor of its masking. She must have been about my age, early forties. She was wearing sober, business-like clothes, with the exception of her shoes, which had small faux-fur tiger-skin stripes on them. We were sitting around a table: Peyman, Tapio, myself, this Minister and two of her staff. The way we were positioned allowed me to see these shoes, and what she was doing with them. As first one, then another person presented, responded, queried, clarified, proposed, counter-proposed and so forth, she rubbed one of her feet against the other, so that her right shoe's toe, its outer edge, moved up and down against the side-arch of its neighbour. She performed this activity non-stop throughout the meeting, even when she herself was talking. I thought at first that she was scratching herself, that she had a bite or irritation on her left foot that was itching. Twenty or so minutes into the meeting, though, I had to abandon this hypothesis: while even low-level scratching has a kind of franticness about it, an angry, stop-start rhythm, her movement was so regular and methodical that it seemed almost automatic. With each upwards motion of the toe against the arch, the tiger-skin, its fur, would be drawn upwards, ruffled until its hairs all separated, each one bristling to attention; with each downward or return stroke these hairs would all lie back flat again, losing their individuality amidst the smooth, sleek flow of feline stripes.

7.4 After the best part of an hour, I realized what this Minister was up to: she was attempting, with her right foot, to undo her left shoe's buckle (which, unusually, fastened on the inward- rather than the outward-facing side). This, I realized as I watched her, was a quite ambitious undertaking. Buckles are finicky; once you remove hands from the equation, mastery of them becomes well-nigh impossible. Yet this is what her right foot, with a persistence and determination that I found increasingly admirable, was trying to do. The buckle had some give in it; the strap had been made pliant by (I presumed) repeated previous attempts to carry out this operation. At the same time, the strap still possessed enough stiffness to ensure that a push applied to its free end caused a whole stretch to be forced up towards—and ultimately through—the metal frame, rather than just crumpling. This didn't, as I mentioned, happen all at once: it took an hour of tiny upward nudges, and of tiny corresponding downward smoothings of the shoe's surrounding surface, for the strap to travel all the way up through the frame's lower side; then, continuing its upward movement even though there was no further *up* for it to go, it snaked back over on itself in such a way that *up* turned into *down* with no perceptible change of direction—and, in performing this manoeuvre, cleared the central bar with all the grace of a pole vaulter, the prong falling away beneath its belly as it did so. Free of all encumbrances, the strap then slipped with rapid ease through the frame's upper side; and *presto!* the operation was completed.

7.5 As if this weren't impressive enough, the Minister then proceeded, using the outside edge of her right shoe's toe once more, to re-do the sequence in reverse. It took the best part of another hour; but she managed it as well. As soon as she'd returned the buckle to its starting position, its original state, she called the meeting to a close. I found the whole experience of observing this small episode, this drama that (due to the shape of the table, its supporting legs, the layout of our chairs and similar factors) I alone could see, deeply satisfying. How do you think it went? Peyman asked me after we had left. Oh, I answered: excellently.

7.6 Back in the office, as our work on the Koob-Sassen Project kicked in and the general traffic-levels edged up, we started experiencing problems with our bandwidth. There was too much information, I guess, shuttling through the servers, down the cables, through the air. My computer, like those of all my colleagues, was afflicted by frequent bouts of buffering. I'd hear Daniel swearing in the next room—*Fucking buffering!*—and others shouting the same thing upstairs, their voices funneled to me by the ventilation system. The buffering didn't bother me, though; I'd spend long stretches staring at the little spinning circle on my screen, losing myself in it. Behind it, I pictured hordes of bits and bytes and megabytes, all beavering away to get the requisite data to me; behind them, I pictured a giant *über*-server, housed somewhere in Finland or Nevada or Uzbekistan: stacks of memory banks, satellite dishes sprouting all around them, pumping out information non-stop, more of it than any single person would need in their lifetime, pumping it all my way in an endless, unconditional and grace-conferring act of generosity. *Datum est:* it is given. It was this gift, I told myself, this bottomless and inexhaustible torrent of giving, that made the circle spin: the data itself, its pure, unfiltered content as it rushed into my system, which, in turn, whirred into streamlined action as it started to reorganize it into legible form. The thought was almost sublimely reassuring.

7.7 But on this thought's outer reaches lay a much less reassuring counter-thought: what if it were just a circle, spinning on my screen, and nothing else? What if the supply-chain, its great bounty, had dried up, or been cut off, or never been connected in the first place? Each time that I allowed this possibility to take hold of my mind, the sense of bliss gave over to a kind of dread. If it was a video-file that I was trying to watch, then at the bottom of the screen there'd be that line, that bar that slowly fills itself in—twice: once in bold red and, at the same time, running ahead of that, in fainter grey; the fainter section, of course, has to remain in advance of the bold section, and of the cursor showing which part of the video you're actually watching at a given moment; if the cursor and red section catch up, then buffering sets in again. Staring at this bar, losing myself in it just as with the circle, I was granted a small revelation: it dawned on me that what I was *actually* watching was nothing less than the skeleton, laid bare, of time or memory itself. Not our computers' time and memory, but our own. This was its structure. We require experience to stay ahead, if only by a nose, of our *consciousness* of experience—if for no other reason than that the latter needs to make sense of the former, to (as Peyman would say) narrate it both to others and ourselves, and, for this purpose, has to be fed with a constant, unsorted supply of fresh sensations and events. But when the narrating cursor catches right up with the rendering one, when occurrences and situations don't replenish themselves quickly enough for the awareness they sustain, when, no matter how fast they regenerate, they're instantly devoured by a mouth too voracious to let anything gather or accrue unconsumed before it, then we find ourselves jammed, stuck in limbo: we can enjoy *neither* experience *nor* consciousness of it. Everything becomes buffering, and buffering becomes everything. The revelation pleased me. I decided I would start a dossier on buffering.

7.8 Bronisław Malinowski, the father of modern anthropology, said: Write Everything Down. That was his First Commandment. You never know (he reasoned) what will turn out to be important and what won't; so capture it all, turn it *all* into data. I used to adhere devoutly to this commandment: as a student, during my clubbing-book research phase, and onwards. I'd keep field-notes which I'd type up in the evening, or first thing in the morning after each night-before: detailed accounts of even—especially—the preceding day's most trivial encounters; impressions of the people and locations these involved; first-pass appraisals of the hue and undertone of situations. When Peyman, with his visionary vagueness, handed me my epic, my epochal, commission, this Great Report, the sense that anything might end up forming part of this made everything I came across, every event I lived through, glow and buzz with potential even more. Paradoxically, though, at the same time, the writing-down, the field-note-taking, tapered off. This wasn't due to lack of commitment—far from it. It was a consequence of Peyman's way of thinking. He didn't, it was quite clear, want a standard ethnographic paper that would sit gathering dust, or cyber-dust, alongside others: he wanted something different and surprising; something bigger, more ambitious and, above all, *new*. It will find its shape, he'd said; I leave all that to you.

This was the exciting part: this remit to leave all established ethnographic protocol behind, to go off-road, off-map, as radical and left-field as I wanted. Anything went. What if . . . ? What if, rather than *it* finding its shape, the age itself, in all its shapeshifting and multi-channeled incarnations, were to find and mold *it*? What if the age, the era, were to do this from so close up, and with such immediacy and force, that the *it* would all but vanish, leaving just world-shape, era-mold? I started to think thoughts like this. They excited me. Beneath their vagueness, I felt something forming—something important and beautiful and momentous.

7.9 One evening, a few months after I'd joined the Company, and about half a year before we won the Project contract, I found myself, still in the throes of these thoughts, drinking with a woman in a bar—a random stranger with whom I'd struck up a conversation. At some point, I stopped listening to what she was saying to me and looked instead at the objects she had placed around her: a cigarette pack, a plastic lighter, a dog-eared travelcard and a key-fob, fanned out in a rough semicircle across the zinc counter, like a spread of cards. She was, like many single women in her situation, using these objects to create a buffer zone around herself, in which her lifestyle, personality and, not least, availability were simultaneously signaled and withheld. I'd bought her a fresh drink; beer-froth was brimming over her glass's rim and running down onto the counter, where it streaked in rivulets between the objects, linking them together as it sogged their edges. Where previously I would have made a mental note of all these objects and then, *à la* Malinowski, written them down later so that each of them could, when analyzed, yield its semantic content (the key-fob had a picture of some elaborately hairstyled space-princess on it, a pre- or proto-Leian heroine dating right back to the days of silent cinema), now I simply looked at them, blurring my vision till my own gaze became soggy and I lost myself among them.

7.10 And as I did, I felt a fragile, almost epiphanic tingling of *what-if*-ness come across me. What if . . . ? What if just *coexisting* with these objects and this person, letting my own edges run among them, occupying this moment, or, more to the point, allowing *it* to occupy *me*, to blot and soak me up, rather than treating it as feed-data for a later stock-taking—what if all this, maybe, *was* part of the Great Report? What if the Report might somehow, in some way, be lived, be *be*-d, rather than written? I didn't go home with this girl, this frothy, streaky, princess-in-a-galaxy-far-away woman, and in fact never saw her again—but that didn't matter. *Fulgurate,* Peyman had said. As I drank with her, and as I left the bar, and over the next days, and weeks, a new field, a new realm, a whole new Order of anthropological experience seemed to burst open and fulgurate before me, its pieces glittering and dancing madly as they started to take up positions within what I suspected might, one day, turn out to be a stable and coherent pattern—an Order of which I, not Malinowski, would be founding father. What if . . . ?

In my reverie, I saw a future where, with my name echoing inside their heads, ethnographers—*U-thnographers!*—no longer scrolling through dead entrails of events hoping to unpack the meaning of their gestures, would instead place themselves *inside* events and situations *as they unfolded*—naïvely, blithely and, most of all, *live*—their participation-from-within transforming life by bringing its true substance to the fore at every instant, in the instant, not as future knowledge but *as* the instant itself, which, like a ripened pod, would overswell its bounds and rupture, spawning meaning, spreading it forth to all corners of the world . . . Then the Great Report would not be something that was either to-come or completed, in-the-past: it would be all *now*. Present-tense anthropology; anthropology as way-of-life. That was it: Present-Tense Anthropology™; an anthropology that bathed in presence, and in *now*ness—bathed in it as in a deep, bubbling and nymph-saturated well.

7.II And yet . . . And yet . . . And yet. The Great Report still had to be composed. That was the deal: with Peyman, with the age. Even if it wasn't composed in a way that conformed to any previous anthropological model, it nonetheless had, somehow, to find a form. It was all a question of form. What fluid, morphing hybrid could I come up with to be equal to that task? What medium, or media, would it inhabit? Would it tell a story? If so, how, and about what, or whom? If not, how would it all congeal, around what cohere? How could I elevate the photos I had pinned about my walls, the sketches, doodles, musings,

all the stuff cached on my hard-drive, the audio-files and dia-
ries not my own—how could I elevate all these from secondary
sources to be quantified, sucked dry, then cast away, to primary
players in this story, or non-story? Above and beyond this, how
could life *as lived* become transmogrified from field-work into
work, *the* Work? Here my thinking, I'll admit, got vague even
by Peyman's standards. What if . . . ? I imagined cells of clan-
destine new-ethnographic operators doing strange things in
deliberate, strategic ways, like those conceptual artists from
the sixties who made careers out of following strangers around
for hours on end or triggering unusual events, specific situations (fainting, or rather pretending to, or simply lying down,
in a busy street, say, or staging a quarrel in a café) . . . Could
that kind of stuff, that kind of practice, be applied to modern
life? And then, *as* Present-Tense Anthropology™, could it be
somehow passed on, communicated to (or even replicated by)
collaborators who might, through the very act of recognizing it,
cause it to be simultaneously registered, logged, archived . . .
Could *that* be it . . . ? How would it work . . . ? I tried to picture
cells, "chapters" of new-ethnographic agents, like you get with
biker-gangs and spies, each of them primed, initiated, privy to
a set of protocols and gestures, that a tacit call to order might
activate, and re-activate time and again . . . And then the rituals
and ceremonies that ensued—might *that* be the Report . . . ?
Would this new Order then, like a cult gestating in the cata-
combs of some great city it will one day come to dominate, pul-
sate and grow with each one of these covert iterations—until,
eventually, it might, yes, *fulgurate:* erupt, break cover, soar

upwards and, in the light of full, unhindered proclamation, found its Church? Then the world would be made over; there'd be jubilation, exaltation: I saw Nobel Prize dinners and ticker-tape parades and general dancing in the streets. But still—here was the catch; here, every time, even my wildest fantasies, with their champagne and bunting and confetti, came back full circle to their sober starting point—for all that to come to pass, for that whole sequence to be set in motion, the Great Report had first, somehow, to come into being.

7.12 The iodine's not getting any traction, Petr said the next time I met him; so they're trying a new tactic. Oh yes? I asked. What's that? Well, he told me, they've taken sample cancer-cells from me and sent them to this lab where they mix them with cells from honey, and thyme, and rosemary, and the sweat of humming-birds, and all kinds of natural things. The cells of these have quite specific structures, which react in certain ways with other structures—and, once in a while, one set of cells can neutralize another, take them out. If they find one that takes out my cells, then we're rolling. Don't they know already which cell-structure will suit you? I asked. No, he replied, they haven't got it all mapped: it's still hit and miss. You just have to pair your cells with each of these others, moving down the line, running the gauntlet, and you never know, you might just find a match. The lab's in Greece, he said. Greece? I asked. Yeah, he answered: Greece. How about that? He paused, and I pictured this Greek lab for a few moments. I had a quite clear picture of it—only it was shedding, even as I held it in my mind, its modern, scientific ambiance and acquiring an ancient one instead: mutating into a grotto full of hecatombs and urns into which white-robed ministers served offerings of blood and flesh. Above these ministers, hovering beyond the smoke and vapour, a pantheon of gods sat around a long board table at whose centre lay a big, fat tome in which all structures and all matches had been written down. It was to them, to this Olympian committee, that these libations were being given, these supplications made—made in the hope that the committee might, in their infinite pity, wisdom and benevolence, do what only they could do: look up an entry and send back to meek, afflicted mortals a celestial *ping!* of recognition. Petr started speaking again, his words floating above this vision like a voice-over. It's worth a try, he said.

7.13 Talking of visions: as time went on, my mental picture of the Project, my baroque casting, or elaboration, of it, changed. Out went the towers and palaces—or rather, better to say they flattened, their balconies and arches, corbels, cornices and spires and all such wedding-cakery steamrollered down into a uniform consistency. What these second-generation reveries gave me in their place, compressed and smooth, was a black box. It might have still been standing in the desert; or perhaps up on a plateau, a raised plain—above a city maybe, like the Parthenon, or maybe situated (for strategic reasons) far from any settlement, but nonetheless connected to a city, or a set of cities, over which it exerted influence. Then again, sometimes this black box in which Koob-Sassen had become embodied seemed to be lying on the shelf of some administrative building. More accurate, perhaps, to describe it as resting on a *plane*, rather than plain: one geometric shape that sat atop another. As to its size: this, too, was far from clear. It was hard, in these visions, to maintain a sense of scale. Sometimes it seemed enormous, like an emperor's mausoleum; at others it appeared no larger than a trunk, or coffin; at others still, the size of a child's toy- or music-box. The only constant or unchanging aspect of it was that it was black: black and inscrutable, opaque.

8.

8.1 And all this time, behind these apparitions, another one: the image of a severed parachute that floated, like some jellyfish or octopus, through the polluted waters of my mind: the domed canopy above, the floppy strings casually twining their way downwards from this like blithe tentacles, free ends waving in the breeze. This last picture, for me, produces, even now, a sense of calm: no angry and insistent tow, no jerks and tugs and stresses—just a set of unencumbered cords carelessly feeling the air. This sense of calm, of languidness, grows all the more pronounced when set against the panic of the man hurtling away from it below. He would have looked up, naturally, and seen the chute lolling unburdened and indifferent above him—as though freed from the dense load of all its troubles, that conglomeration of anxiety and nerves that he, and the human form in general, represented. Considering the picture, I found my focus, my point of identification within it and my attendant sympathy, shifting from the diminutive man to his expanded, if detached, paraphernalia. I felt quite happy for the latter, for its liberation into carefreeness. Parachutes, as a rule, are treated badly by their human masters: granted false release and then immediately yanked back into servitude, into yoked bondage. This one, though, had slipped the bridle—literally—and billowed out into a freedom that was permanent and real. Its existence would have been a good and full one from this moment onwards.

8.2 The following weekend, the newspaper—the old-style broadsheet, I mean—carried a longer, more reflective article about the case. Its author was an occasional skydiver himself. He discussed the culture of the sport, its general fraternity. Skydivers, he informed his readers, are a close-knit bunch. They have, he wrote, the feeling of being *part of a tribe*. This sentence jumped out at me, for obvious reasons; on reading it, I looked up at the byline, to see if I recognized the journalist's name. I didn't. I thought of my Vanuatans once again. In their tower-plunging ritual, the vines, as I mentioned earlier, were measured so as to tauten not in mid-air but rather only fractionally above the earth: the jumps deemed the best, the ones that won the diver most acclaim, were those in which the cords sprang into action *as* he hit the ground, plucking him back from the very jaws of death into which they'd tantalizingly allowed him, for a fraction of a second, to descend. On such perfectly realized jumps, the diver's shoulders would flick leaves and brushwood as they jerked back upwards, as though impudently scrawling the man's signature across the forest floor. The movement was extremely pleasing to observe. It was this act of scrawling, this graffiti-gesture, I now realized, that, above all other aspects of the ritual, had back then made me want to be a tower-plunger, or anthropologist, or both.

8.3 The article kept mentioning "faith." Skydivers are induced into and graduate up through a world in which faith plays a fundamental role. They must believe in their instructors; in the equipment; in the staff packing their rigs; in tiny ring-pulls, clips and clip-releases, strips of canvas, satin, string. It could be argued, wrote the author, that this belief had nothing of the devotional or metaphysical about it, since each of the things to be believed in had a solid evidential underpinning: the mechanics of a ripcord, say, or a spring-loaded riser—or, of course, on a larger scale, the overall infallibility of physics, its laws of resistance, drag and so on. Yet, he claimed, these things could only carry one so far towards a gaping hole in a plane's side, and the fundamentally counterintuitive act of throwing oneself through it: to cite the clichéd but apt maxim, they could take the horse to water, but they couldn't make it drink. That final spur, the one that carried skydivers across the threshold, out into the abyss, was faith: faith that it all—the system, in its boundless and unquantifiable entirety—*worked,* that they'd be gathered up and saved. For this man, though, the victim, that system, its whole fabric, had unraveled. That, and not his death, was the catastrophe that had befallen him. We're all going to die: there's nothing so disastrous about that, nothing in its ineluctability that undermines the structure of our being. But for the faith, the blind, absolute faith into whose arms he had entrusted his existence, from whose mouth he'd sought a whispered affirmation of its very possibility—for that to suddenly be plucked away: that must have been atrocious. He'd have looked around him, seen the sky, and earth, its landmass and horizon, all the vertical and horizontal axes that hold these together, felt acceleration and the atmosphere and all the rest, the fundamental elements in which we hang suspended all the time, whether we've just jumped from an aeroplane or not—and yet, for him, this realm, with all its width and depth and volume, would have, in an instant, become emptied of its properties, its values. The vast font at which he prayed, and into which he sank, as though to re-baptize himself, time and again, would, in the blink of a dilated eye, have been voided of godhead, rendered meaningless. Space, even as he plunged into it, through it, would have retreated—recoiled, contracted, pulled back from its frontiers even though these stayed intact—withdrawn to some zero-point at which it flips into its negative. Negative world, negative sky, negative everything: that's the territory this man had entered. Did that then mean he'd somehow fallen through into another world, another sky? A richer, fuller, more embracing one? I don't think so.

8.4 Why are your walls covered in pictures of parachutes? asked Tapio when he popped his head into my office one day. It's to do with the Project, I told him; its overall . . . configuration. Oh yes? he said in his robotic voice. Yes, I repeated:

there are all these strands, and they converge; and there's an overarching roof—or, let's say, membrane, skin—above them. And, I continued, warming to my theme, what powers the whole thing isn't some internal engine, since it doesn't have one, but rather the way its structure, due to the way it's, you know, structured, generates kinetic energy as everything around it—in this case, the air—passes through it. I see, said Tapio; and he stared intently at the pictures and the words, the lines conjoining them, for a long time, his own mind whirring as its gears engaged with these. The main thing is, I told him, that (unlike a windmill) a parachute functions not in a fixed location but rather *in transit* from a point A (the aeroplane) to a point B (the assigned landing-spot on the ground); although these two points are in fact anathema—or, at least, exterior—to its own operation as a parachute: once the ground-target is attained, the parachute stops playing its role, just as, prior to the jump, it remains undeployed. Well, I continued, same thing with the Project: it has to be conceived of as in a perpetual state of passage, not arrival—not *at,* but *between.* Tapio nodded sagely as I made all this up. Was I lying to him? As I spoke, I didn't even know.

8.5 *Le Dupe.* At one point in *Tristes Tropiques,* Lévi-Strauss recounts his meeting with a tribe who don't know what writing is. This tribe's chief, wanting to maintain his elevated status, takes up one of Lévi-Strauss's pads and starts to scribble on it, figuring that his subjects won't know the difference: he can con them into thinking that he's versed in this activity. I'd often think about this episode as I compiled my dossiers for clients. I also thought, while interrogating my informants, of a later part of *Tristes Tropiques,* in which the subject of duping crops up once more. Having encountered endless tribes who aren't "strange" enough—tribes who, once decoded, lose all their mystique—my hero finally alights, far up some river, on a tribe *so* fucking strange he can't make head or tail of them. This exasperates him too: incomprehensible is no better than banal—it's just its flip-side. But maybe, just *maybe,* he reasons, somewhere in between these two extremes—in between understanding so completely that an object's robbed of its allure (on the one hand), and (on the other one) not understanding anything at all—there might be some "ambiguous instances" in which the balance is just *right.* These instances, he tells us, would be godsends; they'd provide us with the very reasons, or excuses, for our own existence. But wouldn't these instances, too (he asks), be cons? Who's the real dupe of the confusion sown by observations which are carried just far enough to reach the border-line of the intelligible, only to be stopped short there? It's as though he, Lévi-Strauss himself, were now playing the role of the phony, hand-chancing, pen-wielding chief. Will his own subordinates, he wonders—his readers, that is—be taken in? Or is he (*we,* he writes, *nous*)—are we the dupe ourselves, tricked into a situation in which we'll never be satisfied until we've dissipated what he calls a *residue* that keeps our vanity, and us, ticking along?

8.6 Vanuatans have another trademark custom: the Cargo Cult. Unlike Tower Plunging, which dates back centuries, this one has very recent origins. When, during World War Two, the US Army commandeered sections of their island for the war-effort against Japan, they built airstrips. Big cargo planes landed on these, from which not only military hardware but also more mundane objects large and small—cookers, fridges, tinned food and the whole inventory of goods and appliances that supported the Americans' extended presence there—were unloaded. The natives watched the ground crews bring these metal beasts to heel by waving ping-pong bats at them; watched them disgorge, with the help of forklifts and pneumatic platforms, their great stomachs' bounty; watched the spinning radar beacons conjure more and more of them from empty skies; heard, wafting from open control-tower windows, transmissions swimming in a sea of static. For them, all these things appeared to be elaborate rituals, ones whose outcomes were both concrete and desirable. Who wouldn't want a fridge in a tropical climate, or tinned food where foraging and hunting are arduous? When the war ended, the Americans decamped: dismantled all their masts and runways, packed up their fridges, washing machines, record-players and radios, and disappeared into the sky from which they'd first materialized. The Vanuatans, suddenly bereft of all the benefits of Western gadgetry, took consolation in the fact that they had learnt the rites: like anthropologists, they'd studied the bat-waving routines, learnt the choreography of military salutation, noted down the chains of tower-to-pilot scripture, and so on. They had the sequences, the code. Over the following months, and years, and decades, they laid new matted strips down, constructed beacons and antenna-topped control towers, ping-pong bats and forklift trucks alike from balsa and bamboo. And, rotating, waving and generally manipulating these, they enacted, or re-enacted, all the ceremonies that had caused the bounty-laden planes to appear in the first place. If we do it enough, their logic went, the planes will come again. Perhaps not now, or next week, or next month—but one day, they will come.

8.7 The anthropologists who first reported on these cargo cultists treated them with a mixture of amusement and derision. Special chuckles were reserved for the ceremonial name, or title, that was given to the emissary who (it was hoped) would be the first one to return, and whose appearance would herald the onset of a new age of material prosperity: John Frumm. The name, the ethnographers had ascertained through interviewing older islanders, was derived from that of one of the regular cargo handlers or bat-wavers during the golden era of the occupation, who identified himself as simply *John from America*—a name the Vanuatans, in their *patois,* had contracted to John Frumm. But when a second wave of ethnographers came to the island, and revisited, in the light of the new research they conducted there, the first wave's studies, they criticized the colonialist arrogance of their predecessors. More than that: speaking of motes and beams, they urged humility. For hadn't the West also been awaiting a re-arrival from the skies,

and not just for fifty years? Didn't we, too, have our own, Naz-
arene John Frumm? They were, of course, correct. Nor was
this Messianism confined to Christians. It strikes me that our
entire social organism—its economy, its social policy, its civil
order—that these don't implode, hurling us all into a wild abyss
of plunder, rape and burning, is down to their being reined in,
held in alignment, by a yoking to this notion of the Future; and
humanity, its gaze fixed on this apparition hovering just over
the horizon, is thus herded along the requisite channels, its
anarchic inclinations kept in check. Certainly, each brief the
Company worked on, every pitch we made, involved an invo-
cation of, a genuflection to, the Future: explaining how social
media will become the new press-baronage, or suburbia the
new town centre, or how emerging economies would bypass
the analogue to plunge straight into the post-digital phase—
using the Future to confer the seal of truth on these scenarios
and assertions, making them absolute and objective simply *by*
placing them within this Future: that's how we won contracts.
Everything, as Peyman said, may be a fiction—but the Future is
the biggest shaggy-dog story of all.

8.8 They didn't find a match, said Petr, the next time I met
him. Who didn't? I asked. The Greeks, he said; the lab. Bum-
mer, I said. Yeah, he answered; useless fucking humming-
birds. There's one thing, though, they still want to try. What's
that? I asked. Orange juice, he told me. Apparently my cells
twitched, or cringed, or did something or other, when exposed

to Jaffa-orange extract. Not enough to blast them, but enough for them to want to try to flush the bad ones out with orange juice. Flush them out? I repeated. How do they do that? They inject the stuff into my veins, said Petr. They shoot you full of orange juice? I asked. Not any orange juice, he said: they have to be Jaffa oranges, from Israel and the Lebanon, or Gaza, Palestine, the Holy Land—whatever you call that part of the world now. I've got to go, he said a moment later, and took off; but the thought of him being filled with Middle Eastern orange juice stuck with me for a day or two. Where, before, I'd seen Grecian caves and temples, now my mind's eye gave me hot, cracked hillsides on which orange groves were planted. Far from presenting an idyllic landscape, these hillsides and these orange groves were dotted with gun emplacements, capped with observation posts from which surrounding villages could be monitored and showered with mortars. Walls, made not of old stones but of ugly modern concrete topped with barbed wire, hemmed these groves in, cutting some of them in two. Beneath them, and beneath the villages, down in valleys that stretched as far as the eye could see in every which direction, oil wells burned, their smoke-plumes blackening the sky— and blackening the orange groves as well as they drifted across these, leaving tarry deposits on trees' barks, on leaves and on the fruit itself. When that scene came to me, when I pictured all its hatred, all its violence, all its blackness, being injected into Petr, I knew—instinctively and with complete certainty—that he was going to die.

8.9 The day after I met him was a Saturday. Awaking at home to a free diary and no hangover, I sat down at my desk to plan some kind of outline for the Great Report. It was time, I told myself: time to begin this in earnest. Not the Report *per se,* but rather its schema, prolegomena, what-have-you. I installed myself at my desk. It was a good desk; it had cost me quite a bit of money. It had an elegant teak body on whose upper surface sat a leather desktop of a dark-blue tint; set in the leather was a large rectangular writing surface with a blotter backing. That Saturday, I cleared the desktop thoroughly and ruthlessly: every object had to go from it; each notebook, stapler, pencil-holder, scrap of paper; the telephone, the clock (especially the clock); rubbers and paperweights—everything. After I'd cleared it I cleaned it, wiping the leather with a cloth doused in a purpose-made detergent that I'd bought at the same time as I got the desk. One day, I'd told myself, I'll need to clean it properly and thoroughly, transform it into a *tabula rasa* upon which I might compose a great, momentous work. I'd been right: that day was now. I cleaned it, then I dried it with a tea-towel. It was so clean it almost shone—although the darkness of the leather muffled any sheen, reburied this instead inside itself, which seemed, in turn, to give the desktop more intensity, bigger potential as a launch pad for the task at hand. The smell that rose from it was almost natural, like the smell that comes from lawns and meadows when long grass has just been mown. Sitting at it, I looked out of the window at the sky. This was blue too—clear blue with the odd wisp of cloud. I angled myself so as to face the largest uninterrupted stretch of sky, then turned so as to align myself exactly with the desktop, so that the borders and perimeters of this ran parallel and perpendicular to those of my gaze. I sat there for a long time, luxuriating in the emptiness of first one space then the other: desktop, sky, desktop. It was definitely time.

8.10 My window looked out over a rectangular, communal garden within which a pond, also rectangular, was inlaid. Neighbours crossed this garden as they left their flats from time to time. There was a family with two small girls. One of the girls, the younger one, had slipped into the pond a few weeks earlier, between the concrete flagstones that spanned this, and I'd come out of my flat to pull her out. Her parents had brought flowers round the next day. The girl wouldn't have drowned: the pond wasn't very deep, and the mother had arrived on the scene just a few seconds after my sub-heroic intervention. Nonetheless, they'd thanked me, borne me floral offerings. The parents and their daughters passed through the garden today, on the way to ballet class, or so the clothes the rescued daughter and her elder sister wore suggested. Another neighbour came out with a small dog tucked beneath her arm. She wasn't meant to have a dog: the estate was dog-free. She'd had an order served against her, a writ from the corporation, which she seemed to be ignoring. I was torn between annoyance at this old woman for keeping the pet, since this displayed an arrogant disdain towards her other neighbours, not least me; and admiration for her solitary, resolute defiance of the forces of the law which were being brought to bear on her. Was she a rebel or a die-hard bourgeois individualist? I chewed this question over as I sat at my teak and leather desk. The dog was a Chihuahua—barely a dog at all; more like a guinea pig or hamster. Its owner teetered (she'd had a small stroke a year earlier) as she carried it across the garden in a shopping bag, like a degraded version of some Hollywood star. When she'd passed from view I looked back at the empty desktop. How much time had passed? I couldn't tell, since I'd removed the clock. But time had passed. And I was hungry. I decided to go out for lunch; or brunch; or breakfast; whatever. No Report had been commenced, no frame or outline set up, but that was okay. I didn't need to force things. I had staked a claim, made space: that was enough.

8.11 One day the following week, I visited Daniel's office again. This time I found him watching a projection that showed Muslim pilgrims performing the Hajj inside the giant mosque in Mecca. Thousands, tens of thousands, of them knelt and stood in neat, concentric rows; as these static rows converged towards the cube, itself the size of a large building, that lay at the centre of the mosque, they turned into a swirl of slowly moving bodies circling the object. Did you film this? I asked Daniel. No, he said; I found it on the Internet. It had a soundtrack, he said, prayer and music, but I turned it off. You know what this is called? he asked me. No, I told him. *Tawaf,* he said: circumambulation. They move anti-clockwise round the *Kaaba. Anti*-clockwise? I asked. How come? I don't know, he said. Something to do with heavenly bodies: galaxies and planets and the like—some theory of universal movement. We watched some more. As pilgrims shifted from kneeling to standing positions, all in unison, the image's whole texture changed. When, nearer the centre, they all started circling, they became a spinning comet, petals on a flower, bright water flowing down a plughole. At the very centre, the smooth movement met with some resistance as hands reached out to the cube and got some traction on its granite, if just for a second, before being swept onwards as new hands replaced them. The process seemed endless, self-perpetuating: as each static row of white-robed figures was picked up and swept into the swirl, the next row moved up one to take its place, and each row behind this one did the same, a new row forming at the back, more pilgrims waiting behind this, and more behind. The hands grabbed towards the granite passionately, almost desperately, the angles, tautness and extension of the arms beneath them all exuding longing and abandon. We watched, as was our wont, in silence.

8.12 Later that evening I sat down, once more, to plot the framework of my Great Report. The clearing I'd made on my desktop was still there, untouched and un-encroached-on—save by a small, dead moth whose corpse had landed there after whatever parachute it had put its faith in had failed. I swept it aside; and, once again, the space was pristine, perfect, blank. *Tabula rasa:* I pronounced the words aloud as I surveyed the leather, breathing in its smell of cut grass and detergent. Just sitting before it, above it, filled me with a sense of infinite possibility. I pictured myself as an industrialist, viewing a clearing in the forest where his factory would go; or as an urban planner, given *carte blanche* to design from scratch a new, magnificent cosmopolis; a mathematician, a topologist or trigonometrist, contemplating space in its most pure and abstract form; an explorer, sea-discoverer, world-conqueror from centuries gone by, standing at his prow as his dominion-to-be hove into view: this virgin territory that he would shape after himself and make his own. Placing my laptop in the middle—the exact, geometric centre—of this clearing, I opened a fresh document and stretched its borders out until it filled my screen entirely. As I did this, though, just as the document's expanding lower boundary reached the bottom of my screen, my finger momentarily lost contact with the glide-pad; when the finger made contact again, it caused the applications docked invisibly at the screen's base to pop up, impinging on the clean neutrality both of the screen and of my mind. Trying to hide them once more, I accidentally tapped on the docked news page, which slipped from its box, inflating as it rose, like some malicious genie, taking the screen over—and in an instant, all the extraneous clutter, all the world-debris, that I'd so painstakingly eliminated flooded back into the clearing, ruining it.

8.13 The news page carried new news of the oil spill—of the current one, I mean, the one that had been playing out for the last few weeks. The worst-case scenario, the event that the authorities, environmentalists and the oil-company itself most feared, had come to pass: the oil had reached the mainland. The coastline was snowy; more than just snowy, it was completely snow-covered, swaddled in a huge, unbroken blanket of the stuff. The contact between oil and snow, the impact of the former on the latter, was being shown in close-up, from the land, and long-shot, from a plane—but the same effect could be seen in both views. The snow seemed to absorb and drink in the oil in an almost thirsty way: to blot it up, then pass it onwards through its mass, as though, within the architecture of its vaulted and communicating chambers, their crystalline ice-particles, a series of distribution hubs were secreted. Still sitting at my desk, looking down at the laptop, at the picture on its screen, the streaks and clusters taking shape as oil spread slowly inland, I saw ink polluting paper, words marring the whiteness of a page.

9.

9.1 The next week, I flew off to Frankfurt to speak at a conference. It was held in a new, glitzy building: smart-seats, ambient lighting, corporate logos everywhere. The papers delivered there weren't really *papers* as such—more like sales pitches or motivational speeches, each of which, backed by the latest AV software, advanced a "paradigm" for the delectation of assembled delegates. The event was invitational; to be invited was an honour, confirmation that the invitee belonged to the world's very top rank of paradigm-advancement. I was met at the airport by a man holding a card on which my name was neither handwritten nor printed but rather embossed, then dropped at a hotel that boasted not one but two saunas (the first dry, in the Finnish style; the other, in Turkish, wet). The theme of the conference was—for once!—not The Future. It was The Contemporary. This was even worse. It was, of course, a topic to which I'd been giving much thought: radiant now-ness, Present-Tense Anthropology™ and so forth. But I wasn't ready to give all that stuff, all those half-formed notions, an outing. Besides which, I'd started to harbour doubts about their viability. These doubts themselves, I told myself in the days before the conference, were what I'd air. To air the doubt about a concept before airing the concept itself was, I thought, quite intellectually adventurous; it might go down well.

9.2 Talks were limited to fifteen minutes each. The other speakers' PowerPoint presentations moved with sub-second precision from one image to the next as they talked with evangelic zeal of neuroscience, genomics, bio-informatics and a dozen other concepts currently enjoying their moment in the sun. When my turn came, I didn't have any slides or clips. I started by saying that The Contemporary was a suspect term. Better to speak, I proposed, of a *moving ratio* of modernity: as we straddle the dual territories of a present that, despite its directional drive, is slipping backwards into past, and a future that will always remain notional, we're carried through a constantly mutating space in which modernity itself is no more than a credo in the process of becoming "dated," or at least historical. The term *epoch,* I informed my listeners, originally meant "point of view," as in the practice of astronomy; only later, I said, did it start being used to organize the world into fixed periods. This latter use, I argued, was misguided. Instead of making periodic claims which, since they can't be empirically justified, only produce an infinite regress of detail and futile quibbling over boundaries and definitions, we should return to understanding *epoch* as a place from which one looks at things. From that perspective, I went on—the perspective of shifting perspectives—we can still pose the question of the dif-

ference introduced by one day, one year, one decade, in relation
to another. To understand that question fully, though (I concluded), what we require is not contemporary anthropology
but rather an anthropology *of* The Contemporary. *Ba-boom:*
that was my "out." My talk was met with silence, then, when
my audience realized that I'd finished, a smattering of polite
clapping. No one approached me to discuss it afterwards. Later
that evening, in the "wet" or Turkish sauna, I recognized one of
the other delegates. He recognized me too, but broke off eye-
contact immediately before slipping away into the steam.

9.3 While I was in Frankfurt, I dropped in on a friend of
mine who ran the city's anthropology museum. The museum
was housed in two nineteenth-century villas: one for the public
galleries, the other for administration. I met her in her office in
the second; when she picked her coat up and announced that
she would show me the collection, I presumed that we were
heading for the first. But instead she led me to her car, and we
drove for ten or fifteen minutes to an industrial part of town.
There it is, she said, as the car double-bumped over an old
freight-train track. Following her gaze, I saw a concrete bunker
rising up beside the road. We pulled into a docking bay beneath
this building, parked beneath huge arches and got out. Around
us, large as totem poles, parts of old electric circuits lay about:
fuse-boxes, regulators and capacitators, ribbed ceramic insula-
tors and so on. The building used to house a transponder for
the city's transport system, Claudia explained; that, she said,

pointing to the grille that slid by as we took the roomy, doorless lift up to the fourth floor, was a Faraday cage.

9.4 We walked down corridors whose walls, made of the same thick, unpainted concrete as the building's exterior, made me think of those giant sarcophagi they pour around damaged nuclear plants to stop the radiation leaking out, and came to the collection room itself. Huge metal storage units lined one wall of this, with slide-tracks beneath their bases and spoked handles, like the ones they use in submarines or decompression chambers, mounted on their outer ends. Parallel to these, free-standing filing cabinets stretched the room's whole length, with index numbers marked on every drawer. In the room's centre a long, slab-like table lay. A fat male porter, who seemed to have emerged from the walls and cabinets themselves (I hadn't noticed him when Claudia and I entered the room), laid large sheets of fresh tissue-paper across this, then stood to its side, wordlessly awaiting instructions.

9.5 Where do you want to start? asked Claudia, rattling a set of keys. How do you mean? I asked back. We have over fifty thousand objects here, she said. This way (she gestured to a caged door leading off the main room) is Oceania; that way (she gestured to another caged door on the perpendicular wall) is the Americas; and there (she gestured to a third door on the wall facing Oceania) is Africa—take your pick. I don't know, I told her: Oceania. She fished out the appropriate key and led me through to a room as big as the one we'd left, in which rows of older, wooden cabinets stood, one after the other. Through their vitrines I could see clusters of objects: carved whale-bones, arrow-heads, head-dresses, plates, knives, masks. All the objects had inventory numbers painted on them—usually near the bottom, although, on the smallest ones, the number covered almost the entire surface area. Claudia opened a random cabinet, and an overwhelmingly sharp odour forced its way right up my nostrils to my nose's bridge. Naphthalene, she said, seeing me wince.

9.6 She pulled a pair of smooth white gloves on and picked up a woven belt, one of at least twenty lying folded in rows inside the cabinet. The next cabinet she opened had a similar number of small tobacco boxes in it. Why so many? I asked. Why not just one or two? Claudia started to explain that the larger part of the collection came from what, to my ears, sounded like the Great *Sepia* or *Septic* Journey of 1960. The *What* Journey? I asked. Sepik, she repeated. The Sepik is a river in New Guinea. The Museum, she said, sent an expedition up it, to acquire material culture. They stopped off at every village on the river's banks, one after the next, and the natives sold them things. Word spread (she said) from settlement to settlement; as they arrived at each, the tribe would be waiting there with all their tribal objects laid out, like a jumble sale. The expedition bought so many objects that they filled whole boats and trains with them, stacked up in giant containers. The idea was that you needed to study the morphology of, say, a cooking pot: how the shape and decoration varies from one village or one family to the next. That's why you needed twenty, fifty, a hundred. And, of course, she added, you could trade surplus objects with other anthropology museums back in Europe later: we'll swap you ten head-rests for two totems. The prevailing wisdom was that you had to gather *everything:* a hammer or a pair of scissors might tell you as much about a culture as a sacred fetish—suddenly release its inner secrets, like some codex.

9.7 Claudia paused. When she continued speaking, her voice went strangely melancholic. But then, she said, all that changed. How? I asked. Well, she said, from the mid-sixties, there was a turn away from objects: suddenly the prevailing wisdom held that you don't need to look at pots and arrows anymore—you need to study patterns of behaviour and belief and so forth: *your* school of anthropology, U. She cast an angry glance at me. Trapped with her in this bunker, this cage to which she alone held the keys, I didn't argue back. She took my silence as an admission of guilt, and sighed. Plus, she carried on in a more conciliatory tone, we Europeans started to suspect that it had been a bit shitty to take all these objects in the first place. So now, she said, sweeping her white glove, already a little smudged, round the room, we've got these store-rooms full of crap we'll never show, or even understand. What do you think, for example, she asked, opening another cabinet and pulling out a strange wicker contraption, this thing is for? A snow-shoe? I suggested. U., she said, it's from the tropics. Then a fishing net, I tried again. Maybe, she said. A fishing net; ceremonial head-gear; a bat for playing some kind of game; a cooking implement . . . Who knows? We don't. We won't. We haven't even catalogued half this stuff. What should we do with it? Why not return it? I asked. That doesn't work, she answered curtly. The tribe's descendants don't know what this wicker thing is for either; they've all got mobile phones and drink Coke. And besides, if you repatriate an object it just turns up on the market six months later—may as well just send it straight to the collector's Texas ranch. That's even worse than us having it. So they pile up here. She cast her glance first one way, then another, down the rows of cabinets, and we stood in silence for a moment. Sometimes, she said eventually, I feel like I'm in the final scene in *Raiders of the Lost Ark*, where they stash the holy relic in a box exactly like all the other boxes in some warehouse that just stretches to infinity. Or *Citizen Kane:* same thing, but the artifacts are heading for the fire. This, she said, sweeping her now-dirty glove around once more, isn't fire; but it's oblivion all the same. And all the time, she added, her voice going really quiet, as though she were afraid of being overheard, in the back of my mind I've got the nagging suspicion that one of these objects—just *one*—has *Rosebud* written on its base.

9.8 Before we left the Oceania room, Claudia showed me a large wooden dish across whose surface hundreds of red and white dots had been painted in a semi-regular pattern. These are from Australia, she said. The Aborigines made them. They're sacred. More than sacred: they're hermetic. The dots form a kind of cipher, whose key only a handful of the most senior elders are allowed to know. The younger ones can't even *see* these dishes, let alone be let in on the key. The dishes were brought here in the forties, by an anthropologist: a German one, son of a Lutheran missionary who'd taken his family out there in the twenties. When the son brought these back to Frankfurt, Claudia explained, he set about cracking the cipher. Did he succeed? I asked. He did, Claudia answered. Look. She led me over to a nearby shelf, pulled out a book and flipped through its pages till she came to one on which the very dish she was still holding in her hand was drawn. On the page facing the drawing was a breakdown of the pattern of the dots, and, under that, what I presumed (the book was in German) was an explanation or translation of the text the dots embodied. This, said Claudia, is *their* codex. When the last Aborigine who understood the cipher died without passing the knowledge down, they sent a delegation here, to see this book. It served as a kind of cheat-sheet for them. It was a weird scene: we had all these Aborigines here, wearing their ceremonial garb, walking around Frankfurt. They were grateful to the museum, she continued—although, after they'd looked at the book, they requested that all copies be destroyed. How many copies were there? I asked. Not that many, she said. It was privately printed.

Maybe twenty. They tried to buy them all up, on the Internet, but found that almost all of them were held in obscure libraries, or museums like this one. And what about this copy? I asked. How did you respond to their request? The issue's unresolved, she told me. As for the dishes themselves, they were quite adamant that these must never be shown publicly. I shouldn't even be showing this one to you. In fact, being female, I shouldn't even be holding it. But you are, I said. Yes, she answered, I suppose I am.

9.9 While we were back in the main room, looking at a big sculpted figure that the fat, silent porter, on Claudia's instructions, had lifted from one of the sliding storage-units and laid on the slab for us, Madison called me on my mobile. How on earth does a signal find its way through all this concrete? I asked Claudia. The Faraday cage's metal acts as an aerial, she said. Who are you talking to? asked Madison. I'm looking at a totem pole, I said. That turns me on, said Madison. I looked down at the figure laid out on the white tissue beneath us. It was some kind of warrior-god, garish, daubed in yellow, black and scarlet, with a phallus stretching from his waist up to his chin; his face was twisted in an obscene leer. It's like an alien autopsy, isn't it? Claudia was saying, while Madison elaborated sex scenarios involving poles and savages. Listening to her, I started getting a hard-on, straining at the fabric (denim— selvage) of my trousers. Claudia didn't notice, but the mute porter did.

9.10 As we drove back to the museum, we traded news about our contemporaries from university. A third of them had gone to the developing world, to work for NGOs; another third were, like me, working in the corporate sector; the remaining third were academics. Claudia was the only one to have involved herself with what she again called *material culture*. As we crossed a bridge in the city's centre, I could see, on one side of the river, the new headquarters of the European Central Bank being built; on the other, in a row, the town's museums—all of them: architectural, cinematic, natural-historical and so on—housed, like the anthropological one, in old villas. Further away, spires of cathedrals that had somehow survived wartime blitzing poked out above modern glass and metal. One of the huge cranes building the Bank's HQ was turning as we drove; the box from which the cables carrying the crane's load descended was sliding along the jib-arm, which itself was swinging horizontally across the air. The box was sliding fast, and the arm was swinging fast, and we were driving fast as well; and it appeared, just for a moment, that the box, though hurtling along the moving arm, was staying quite still, rooted to a single spot of air. But only from the speeding car, there on the bridge.

9.11 On the flight back to London, as the stewardess gave me a cup, or I removed a teaspoon from its packet, or folded down and up the tray-table in the seat-back just in front of me, the term *material culture* played and replayed itself in my mental airspace, like a snatch of a stuck record. I couldn't help but see these things—this table, teaspoon, cup—as tribal objects. Also adjustable air-conditioning nozzles, slide-down blinds, Velcro-fitted head-rest covers, motion-sickness bags, buttons with human icons on them and the like. Aliens, after all trace of us has disappeared bar the small handful of our corpses they'll preserve for intermittent laying out on their tissue-coated slabs, will have whole bunkers full of these things, stuffed into naphthalene-laced cabinets, twenty of each spilling out of every drawer, and wonder what the fuck they were all for. Before we'd left the building, Claudia and I had ducked into the other two rooms, those housing the artifacts from the Americas and Africa. These rooms had been similarly crammed with objects—drums and bracelets, loincloths, *Día de los Muertos* figurines—but in the second room, the Africa one, a particular item had held my attention more than all the others. It wasn't, properly speaking, an item: just a lump of some black substance, all unformed, whose rugby ball–sized mass consisted of no more than tubers and protuberances knotted and gnarled together every which way. It's *caoutchouc,* Claudia had said, seeing me staring at it: rubber, in its raw form. Now, looking through the window at the bulbous clouds that, once again, were slightly smudged, I thought of this *caoutchouc;* then of Petr's cancer; then, once more, of spilled oil.

10.

10.1 I spent most of the next week honing in my head the presentation that I *should* have given back in Frankfurt. Consider, gentlemen, the Oil Spill. Oil spills considered as. Considered as a function of or symbol for. When, gentlemen, we consider. No: Consider, then (yes, *then,* like the consideration followed naturally from the preceding one—although there wasn't a preceding one: the proposition just confirmed itself, which made it irrefutable)—consider, then, the Oil Spill. Any oil spill. There's always one happening . . . In my mind's eye, the hi-tech modern conference hall morphed into a nineteenth- or even eighteenth-century auditorium: steep-banked rows of wooden benches, an audience made up exclusively of men with bushy sideburns and high collars, pipe- and cigar-smoke mingling with murmurs of approval in air already thick with erudition and just plain old age—although I still had a projector wi-fi'd to a sensor on my index finger, split-second responsive . . .

10.2 There's always an oil spill happening, I'd say. Which is why. That's the reason, gentlemen. Which, gentlemen, is the reason we can name it in the singular: *the* Oil Spill—an on-going event whose discrete parts and moments, whatever their particular shapes and vicissitudes (*vicissitudes!* I'd susurrate the word time and again), have run together, merged into a continuum in which all plurals drown. *Click*. Here, gentle-men, you see a tanker trailing its long, black tail. *Click*. Here are vinyl-coated rocks; and here—*click*—a PVC-hemmed coast-line. Nature got up in her fetish gear, her gimp-outfit. *Click*. Here's one showing men with body-suits and gloves pacing a taped-off beach the way forensic detectives do at crime scenes. *Click*. Here's a video-file: a close-up sequence, captured by a hand-held underwater camera, of a few feet of seabed. Note the way the semi-hardened oil stretches and folds as the div-er's hand lifts it. Can you see the look on his face? Come, now, come: of course you can. It is the fascinated look your own one had when, as a child, you stood (didn't you?) rooted to the pavement in front of a candy-store window in which taffy was being pulled, transfixed by the contortions of the unman-ageably huge lump—what child, I ask you, gentlemen, could eat all *that*?—as the machine's arms plied it, its endless meta-morphoses as. Stretched and folded, stretched and slapped. Alchemy. Metamorphosis. Material culture.

IO.3 I worked on this imaginary presentation during down-moments: while I was walking around, say, or taking a bath, or staring at Madison's ceiling after sex, or at my office's wall during intervals between two bits of proper work—in other words, pretty much all the time. Oil, gentlemen, I'd say, is hydrophobic: it recoils from water. This is not a tendency or quirk of oil: it is an elemental property that defines it at its very core, shaping its micelles, hydrocarbons, atoms. Oil and water, as the old adage goes, do not mix. So what are we observing when we watch these elements con. When we watch them introduced to. When we watch these liquids thrown together? You might say that we're observing ecological catastrophe, or an indictment of industrial society, or a parable of mankind's hubris. Or you might say, more dispassionately, that we're observing a demonstration of chemical propensities. But the truth is that, behind all these episodes. Dramas: beneath these. Beneath all these dramas, I'd say, and before them, we're observing, simply (gentlemen), differentiation. Differentiation in its purest form: the very *principle* of differentiation. Ones and zeros, *p* and *not-p:* oil, water. Behind all behaviour, issuing instructions, sending in the plays—just as behind life itself, its endless sequencing of polymers—there lies a source-code. This is the base premise of all anthropology.

10.4 At this point in these scripted fantasies, I'd pause to take a sip of Evian, or some such. There'd be a hush as delegates waited for me to carry on. A gesture to the screen as I'd name, once more, the substance filling it: Oil—then, smiling, I'd sweep my hand back towards the bottle, and say: Water. The theatrical manoeuvre sucked them in completely: they were mine. Where one is, I'd tell them, the other cannot be. When we encounter, then, as we do often after spills—*click*—an oily sea, a sea whose body, while it still performs the functions and ceremonies of a sea—flowing, lapping, breaking into waves and the like—has become dark and ponderous, what we're in fact encountering is not a sea at all. It's oil that has ousted the sea, usurped it, packed it off into exile and assumed its position. It's a *putsch*, a *coup d'état*. Another pause to let the metaphor take hold. And yet, I'd say (unpacking it into full-blown conceit now), the usurper has kept all the infrastructure of the *ancien régime* in place, the rules and regulations governing its rhythms and activities. The judiciary and legislature have decided, for their own tactical reasons—for even minerals, gentlemen, display an instinct for self-preservation—to comply fully with the new executive: the same laws of gravity and motion apply as did before; the same day-to-day, minute-to-minute patterns play out as on any other day and as at any other minute; and for many subjects (low-level constituents whose collective toil produces currents, eddies, tides) there's no sign that the *coup* has taken place at all. If they do know, they don't seem to mind; they even seem to welcome the regime-change. And why shouldn't they? It's an improvement. Oil has more consistency than water: it is denser, more substantial—and thus brings the latter into its own more fully, expressing the sea's splendour in a manner more articulate, more something. In a manner more poetic. No, more lyrical: the sea's splendour in a manner far more lyrical than that in which the original ever did. When you watch swell and surf rolling through a sea that's turned to oil, is it not like watching the whole process in slow motion?

All the grace of a wave rendered through high-end visual software that manages to hold and frame each moment without interrupting or arresting. Something to do with sport: when you can see the football's backspin. And the net's grid, exploding. Perfection.

10.5 A swell would, every time, be building up inside the hall at this point in the lecture, nods and murmurs turning into exclamations of excitement; and I'd ride it into the next sentence, leaning forward on my podium. Thus, gentlemen, I'd say, the ocean's choreography, which for so long has held such fascination for us, is made sharper, more momentous: it is amplified. With this word, *amplified,* the swell would break into a foaming, multi-voiced cry of *huzzah!,* surging down the banked rows towards me. Letting it wash past me, then holding its edge back again by raising my wi-fi-enabled finger, I'd continue: The same goes for all those animals you see—*click*—on stricken beaches: tar-drenched birds who float bewilderedly in blackened rock-pools, or—*click*—stare out stoically from atop tarry boulders. Robbed of flight, immobilized, humiliated in an almost ritual manner (and doesn't the inversion make the custom even crueler? Feathers first, *then* pitch!), they become instant martyrs—and, in so becoming, are infused with all the pathos and nobility of tragic heroes. Living Pompeiians! Victims of the oil Gorgon! They, too, are improved—yes, gentlemen, *improved:* augmented, transformed into monumental versions of themselves, superior by the same token as statues are bigger, better versions of historic people. Even the rocks on which they perch are granted status and significance by having their forms so meticulously re-molded by the oil that duplicates them half a centimetre beyond their own mass's natural boundary. Ask any sculptor: to recast even the dullest object is to celebrate it, to align it with its essence at the very moment this emerges, becomes manifest. Has oil not done this to these rocks? Of course it has, with a panache that's the more brilliant for its simplicity: it has made them rockier.

10.6 At this point in my speech a lone, indignant figure in the auditorium's back row would pipe up: *Shame, sir! Shame!* The atmosphere would tense up: a dissenter! I would peer over my glasses, see the wheel-mounted carry-on bag standing at my critic's side and immediately recognize him: it was my old neighbour from Turin—suit on, tie off—bemoaning in his best Eurozonese this spectacle of nature's defilement; denouncing my aestheticizing of it. Me? I'd ask him, glancing exaggeratedly around and behind me for effect; *I'm* "aestheticizing" it? Gentlemen, I'd reason, opening my arms up to my serried ranks of allies; was it not *he* who first used the term *tragedy*? Cheers, rising from hundreds of chests in unison, drowned out his protests: the exchange in the transit lounge was universal knowledge; they all knew that I was right. Who, I'd continue, cast the first aesthetic stone? The truth is, that these people's (for behind this man there lay a much larger constituency: they'd be there, too, dotted about the streets around the conferencing centre, and in homes throughout the city, and in other cities, purchasing ecologically sourced products, sponsoring zoo animals and so forth)—these people's entire mindset is a product of aesthetics. Bad aesthetics, at that: misguided and ignorant. They dislike the oil spill for the way it makes the coastline look "not right," prevents it from illustrating the vision of nature that's been handed down from theologians to romantic poets to explorers, tourists, television viewers: as sublime, virginal and pure. Kitsch, I tell you (here I'd thump my fist onto the podium, three times in quick succession): kitsch, kitsch, *kitsch!* And wrong: for what is oil *but* nature? Rock-filtered organic compounds—animal, vegetable and mineral—broken down and concentrated by the planet's very crust: what could be purer than that? When oil splatters a coastline, Earth wells back up and reveals itself; nature's hidden nature gushes forth. The man who brings this gushing-forth about—the drunk ship's captain, oversightful engineer or negligent safety officer, or, behind these, the oil magnate, or, behind even him, the collective man whose body, faceless and compound as oil itself, is the corporation—*he* should be considered a true environmentalist: nature's more honest intermediary, its loyaler servant. The cheers, at this point, grew quite deafening; the argument was won; and my foe would be evicted from the building, whimpering as blows rained down on him.

10.7 The atmosphere inside the auditorium was, by now—each time—ecstatic. With the casting-out of this sad bleater, a new society, bound in brotherhood of truth and love of oil spills, had been founded. In anticipation of this moment, I'd cued up a second video-file that showed dead fish lolling around congealed oil on the sea's floor. The slowness of this scene (it had been edited by Daniel for maximum effect) was lulling, soothing. Look, I'd say in a quiet voice after we'd all watched the footage, mesmerized, in silence for a while; look at these fishes' eyes. They're black and opaque. And rightly so: for aren't eyes windows to the soul? If you cut open these fish—ichthyomancy, I believe, is the correct. In former times, the appellation for this would have been. Wolfskin-clad men who. If you cut open these fish, you would find oil inside their liver, kidneys, brain and heart. It's what's most intimate to them—what, of them, has survived. Look at the mild underwater current roll them slightly one way, then another. See how their bodies seem to merge with the black mass, then to emerge from it again: belly, gill or tail-edge first, producing strange, outlandish, not-quite-fish shapes. Does it not look as though they were regressing to some previous stage in the evolutionary cycle—not just their own, but that of the whole universe? To some *interim* state of mutation, one in which all forms are up for grabs? Dice in the air, the roulette ball still zipping round the wheel's rim: anything is possible! God's first act, we are told, was to conjoin and divide as he moved through the waters. This, then, is the primal deed replaying itself—but godlessly, driven and orchestrated by the whims of matter alone. It's all the more sacred for that, gentlemen, because all the more true. Nature is senseless. And nature is dirty.

10.8 My fifteen minutes? I'd say, noticing the organizer in the wings, hidden from the audience's view but not from mine, fidgeting with his watch or walkie-talkie, the next scheduled speaker standing awkwardly beside him. What is a quarter-hour, or century, compared to this? Is not the flow of oil the flow of time itself: slowly but inevitably crawling, in a series of identical, repeating pulses, to some final shoreline? It *embodies* time, contains it: future, present, past. How many epochs (with this word I'd pause, as though distracted by the slight, fleeting intrusion of some parallel universe, before pawing the thought away)—how many epochs of pre-history are lodged in this Paleozoic ooze? What back-catalogues of Vendian biota, proto-Cnidarians and Ediacara, their amalgamated urolites and coprolites and burrows, their trace-fossils? To genuinely contemplate, gentlemen, even the smallest drop—to attend to it faithfully, exhaustively—would be to let time expand beyond its Ordovician and Precambrian borders, till it overflowed all measurable limits. When oil spills, Earth opens its archives. That it takes the form of vinyl when it hardens is no chance occurrence; what those men in body-suits on beaches should be doing is not brushing it away but lowering a needle to its furrows and replaying it all, and amplifying it all the while to boot: up and up, exponentially, until from littoral to plain to mountain, land to sky and back to sea again, the destiny of every trilobite resounds. Thank you. Thank you. I'd step back from the lectern and begin to leave the podium, but the cheering would be so clamorous that I'd be forced to come back time and again, to take another bow. Delegates would be surging forwards, address books open, business cards stretched out towards me, their numbers overwhelming the security personnel who tried to hold them back. Thank you, I'd say. Thank you. Thank you once again. I'll see you in the sauna. Thus passed the week.

II.

II.I Sensational development in the skydiving murder case: the police (the following week's news pages informed their readers) had arrested one of his pall-bearers. The suspect, the victim's best friend, had been on the same dive. They'd been inseparable; the suspect had even been the best man at his wedding. No more details could be given at this point: the thing was presumably *sub judice*. There was, however, one more sentence tagged on at the end; a sentence that, while seemingly just factual and neutral, managed to imply a wealth of supposition. It announced that the dead parachutist's wife, herself also a parachutist, was "helping police with their enquiries." The insinuation, of course, was that she'd colluded with the pall-bearing best man—who, it would follow, was her lover. A love-triangle, elevated from the altar to the sky! I marked its various vectors on my walls: lines linking *DP* (Dead Parachutist) to *BM* (Best Man) to *W* (Wife); and each of these to *H1* (Harness One), *H2*, *H3*; and *SR* (Storage Room) to *AP* (Aeroplane); *BR1* (Bedroom One, the conjugal one) to *BR2* (its adulterous counterpart) . . . It was more than just a triangle: it was a web, a tangle of competing sections, intersections, blind spots, unfolding like so many strands till now compressed and hidden in a parachute's sealed bridle; lines that eventually converged, like cords descending from a canopy, on a single spot at my diagram's base—a spot that represented, naturally, not love but death.

11.2 A trip to Stockholm helped bring into focus a small insight I'd had into Madison, the workings of her mind. Each time I'd been abroad, she'd phoned me, full of lust and longing, to demand my swift return; yet, whenever I'd actually been with her, this lust and longing had been missing. We'd had sex, of course, but even then she'd given the impression of being absent, somewhere else. Each time we did it, I'd watch her face. Her eyes would remain closed for most of the encounter; then, as she approached her orgasm, they'd open. But that didn't mean she'd look at me, or at anything else for that matter: as her eyelids slid up, the eyes themselves would roll up with them, and continue rolling after the lids had stopped, until their centres, those small circles of intelligence and colour that you think of as the apertures leading to what's behind the eyes, to their owner's being or essence or whatever, were almost completely occluded—just two small, gelatinous segments remaining, moons of pupil thumbnailed by the overlay of skin. Each time this happened (and it happened every time), I'd find myself transported back to Turin Airport: to that laptop screen on which her face had first appeared and then been frozen in mid-gesture. The expression was the same. It got so that I felt I was penetrating not *her* but rather, *through* her, that other moment:

that long, stretched-out moment, its endless buffering. I would think, again, about the shroud, the not-Christ figure's up-turned eyes; and I'd remember Madison telling me that she, too, had visited that airport, back in 2001, and her not answering my question as to how this came about. The result, the upshot of this repeating cluster of associations, was that Turin, Torino-Caselle, took on over time a kind of sacred aspect: this airport, this slow-spinning hub, this thorn-crown of delay, became, for me, the site of a divine mystery. Approaching and re-entering it, crossing, time after time, its portal, I, too, would become lost in spasms of paralysis.

11.3 In the basement next to me that week, Daniel was watching pretend zombies. They marched across his wall on one of those parades; lurching slowly through the streets, their heads lolling from side to side, their eyes, like Madison's and the video-file's fishes', vacant. There were young ones, old ones, even children taking part. Some wore business clothes, some military uniforms, others firemen's outfits, evening gowns, tracksuits, pyjamas. There were nurses, bridal couples, traffic wardens, fast-food restaurant workers, skateboarders, mothers with zombified babies, hospital patients, clowns. Some of these pretend zombies carried pretend brains, or hearts, or limbs, which they would gnaw at intermittently. Stewards in yellow jackets, themselves daubed in pretend blood, kept the procession to one side of the road, away from traffic. The odd mounted policeman could be seen as well. The pretend zombies lurched past offices and cafés, across traffic intersections, petrol-station forecourts, bridges, civic squares. What city's that? I asked Daniel. What does it matter? he replied. They have zombie parades everywhere now.

II.4 Then, after holding and questioning him for forty-eight hours, the police released the pall-bearing best man. They sprung him without charge, making it clear that they no longer thought he was in any way accountable for his friend's death. In his place, though, they arrested a second member of the club. This one, also well-known to victim, wife, best friend and all, hadn't been on the dive; but he'd had access to the room in which the rigs had all been stored. They also held and questioned him for two days—then released him, once more without making any kind of charge. Over the next two weeks they made four more arrests, each of which ended in an unconditional discharge. They arrested the club secretary; then a senior instructor; then the cleaner; then a member of the canteen staff. Eventually they stopped making arrests: presumably they'd run out of people to slap cuffs on. They started looking down the suicide route instead: exploring the possibility that the victim had sabotaged his own chute. This, too, proved a false trail: the man turned out to have been happy, and to have shown no melancholic tendencies. After this, the whole thing started going quiet; news pages and newspapers all dropped the story. To plug the gap this left in my life, I transferred my attention to the skydiving mysteries in Canada and Poland and New

Zealand. Nobody in the media seemed to have noticed, or at least attributed any significance to, the fact that the episode, its variants, were appearing concurrently on three separate continents. This, too, excited me: that I alone was starting to pick up the outline of a set of permutations, to discern a morphology at work. I say "concurrently," but in fact the overseas cases weren't quite in kilter with the British one: they lagged slightly behind it, and one another. Nonetheless, a similar sequence was playing out in each: a flurry of arrests and speculation, then a dwindling away as all the trails turned cold.

II.5 The Great Report. In *Tristes Tropiques*, Lévi-Strauss recounts how, after spending months on end among the Nambikwara, with no prospect of escape in sight (the rainy season, rivers flooded and un-navigable, all the perks he'd brought with him—food, wine, bottled water, cigarettes—consumed or traded off, clothes damp and rotten as the hut whose dripping walls and ceiling beat out the slow, metronomic rhythm of his days), bored out of his skull and starting to fall prey to what he later called a "mental disorder" that can afflict anthropologists, he started to compose an epic drama. For six days my hero wrote from morning till night on the back of sheets of paper containing his research notes. The drama's plot involved a Roman emperor and his assassin, and a grand exploration of the themes of glory, power, nature and annihilation. I picture him writing it, cold and rheumatic on interminable afternoons. No, scratch that: what I actually picture is the *paper* that he writes it on: on one side, columns of Nambikwara words and phrases, transcriptions of tattoos, diagrams of the village's huts' layout, with attempts to correlate these with the tribe's wider myth and kinship structures, which he's extrapolated and laid out in graphs and tables—then, on the other side, the play. On one side, scientific, evidence-based research; on the other, epic art. If my Report had come to be completed, which side of the paper would it have been written on? More to the point: to which side does this not-Report you're reading now, this offslew of the real, unwritten manuscript, belong? Perhaps to neither side, but to the middle: the damp, pulpy mass that forms the opaque body at whose outer limits, like two mirages, the others hover.

11.6 You still haven't told me how you came to be in that airport, I said to Madison as we lay in bed one evening. There's lots of things I haven't told you, she replied. If people were to tell other people everything about themselves, we'd live in a dull world. If *knowing* everything about a person were the be-all and end-all of human interaction, she said, we'd just carry memory-sticks around and plug them into one another when we met. We could have little ports, slits on our sides, like extra mouths or ears or sex organs, and we'd slip these sticks in and upload, instead of talking or screwing or whatever. Would you like that, Mr. Anthropologist? No, I told her; I don't want to know everything about you. This was true: I hadn't asked her very much about herself at all—her family, her background, any of that stuff—not back in Budapest when we'd first met, and not since, either. Our liaison had been based throughout on minimum exchange of information. I don't want to know everything about you, I repeated. I just want to know what you were doing in Turin. I wasn't in Turin, she said again. Torino-Caselle, I replied; whatever. Why? she asked. I'm intrigued, I told her. What, professionally? she goaded me. That's right, I said: professionally. Well then you'll have to pay me, she said.

II.7 Back at my flat, over the following week, objects started impinging on my desktop clearing. At first it was coffee cups; then letters, which brought bills and take-away menus in their wake; then, once these had pitched camp on the leather, plates of half-eaten food and handkerchiefs and random pocket-contents came blithely by and stayed, since I no longer had the will to evict them. It wasn't laziness, but something much worse. I'd begun to suspect—in fact, I'd become convinced—that this Great Report was un-plottable, un-frameable, un-realizable: in short, and in whatever cross-bred form, whatever medium or media, *un-writable*. Not just by me, with my limited (if once celebrated) capabilities, but fundamentally, essentially, inherently un-writable. It wasn't just the fact that there could no more be a Lévi-Strauss 2.0 than a second Leibniz; beyond this, I grew exasperated every time I tried to picture, even in the most abstract of ways, a mechanism capable of managing and arresting, let alone pinning down and *mapping* the dynamics, processes and patterns—social, anthropological, historical, micro- and macro, what-you-will—that the Report would have to somehow turn into its content, these entities that kept proliferating every which way, from every which turn and juncture, at every which moment. My exasperation led me, each time, to the same conclusion: that it simply wasn't possible. Peyman, it struck me, must have known this; he was too clever not to. Why, then, had he commissioned it from me? Paranoid thoughts started popping up inside my head. I pictured Peyman back, once more, with all his moguls, mover-shakers and connectors, laughing at me, laughing at the thought that I could have believed, even for a moment, he was *serious* . . . Even when I reasoned these last, deranged notions back out to the fringes of my mind, I was still left with the immovable fact of the thing's un-writability. This filled me with anger, and a feeling of stupidity, and sadness, too—grief not for an actual loss but, worse, for a potential or imaginary one: this beautiful, magnificent Report; this book, *the* Book, the fucking Book, that was to *name* our era, *sum it up;* this book that left the format of the book itself behind, this book-beyond-the-book; and, beyond even this, the tantalizing and elusive possibility of transubstantiated now-ness, live-ness it was to inaugurate—the possibility, that is, of Present-Tense Anthropology™. All that was gone. Which, in turn, raised the question: What was *I* still there for?

11.8 Christmas came and went. Parties; provincial exile; a return to London more relieved than joyous; more parties. On the 1st of January I found myself sitting, once more, beside my desk and blotter, looking through the window at the dawn. I always wake up early after drinking. It was a clear dawn, a good one to usher the new year in. The first phase of the Project would be going live this year. I looked at the pond, this site (since I'd rescued the girl there) of a minor resurrection, and thought of Vanuatans once again. On New Year's Day, the men ride out on horses or just run about a stretch of pasture firing arrows up into the air: straight up, more or less vertically. The arrows, naturally, fall back down, with pretty much the same velocity as that with which they flew up in the first place. The men ride or run around until an arrow lands on one of them and kills him. Then they stop: the ritual demands that one man must be taken every year. Hungover, jaded, generally uninvigorated by the world, I found myself, in reverie, wishing— just as I had as a child when jumping from my sisters' bed—that I could be one of these Vanuatan warriors, galloping about the fields, new-year's wind biting at my cheeks, death whistling all around me, whistling me to life . . .

II.9 Still sitting at my desk and blotter, I looked up at the sky and thought these thoughts. At the same time, I thought about my parachutist once again—with the result that the two scenarios, the Vanuatan new-year arrow-shooting ritual and the fatal sky-diving escapade, merged into one. And suddenly, as though out of the sky itself, with all the speed and penetration of an arrow hurtling to earth, a major revelation came to me. In that instant, I saw the truth behind the parachutist case with

total clarity: it was a Russian Roulette pact! The members of
the club, or at least a clique within their larger congregation,
had made an illicit deal among themselves. No longer satisfied
with the adrenaline-hit they got from simply jumping from
a plane, they'd upped the stakes, the ante, upped them to the
biggest one imaginable, by secretly agreeing to sabotage a single parachute and throw it back into the general pile of packs.
No one would know which pack they'd sabotaged, since they
all looked the same. And there'd always be surplus packs, of
course: the bad one might lie around unused for a year, two
years, forever. Or, of course, it might be used at any time: on
this jump, right now . . . They'd never know: that's why they
did it, just like Russian Roulette players. I was certain of this.
I was more certain of it than of anything before or since. The
triangles, the lines and vectors all made sense now: it seemed to
me, in that instant, that I'd solved not just a private puzzle but
a fundamental riddle of our time. And not just a single riddle
either: the Canadian case, the Polish and New Zealand ones—
these, I was certain, were Russian Roulette pacts as well. It was
a cult, dispersed, like my own covert anthropologists, around
the globe! The realization was enormous—almost as visceral
as the ritual it unmasked. It made the blood rush suddenly to
my head as I shouted *Fuck! Fuck!*—not in anger but in awe;
to no one, in the middle of my living room: the same reaction
I'd had when I watched the Twin Towers falling down on live
TV. I paced about quite frantically; I couldn't sit, or even stand
still. What to do with this incredible knowledge? Go to the
police? It was bigger than that, bigger than solving a crime; big-

ger even than the (now-defunct) Great Report. I'd made a genuine *discovery*, a breakthrough, on the scale of Schrödinger's or Einstein's. Of this I was quite certain. *Fuck!* I shouted, one more time; then I sat down, shot through with revelation. The year would be a glorious one.

12.

12.1 Petr was admitted to hospital in mid-January. The cancer had spread all round his body. It was particularly bad in his lungs. They'd started to fill up with fluid, which meant he couldn't really breathe. So the doctors had drilled holes in his chest to drain the fluid out through. When I visited him, in a ward full of people who were obviously dying, he was propped up in a bed with these tubes leading from his chest (one from each side) towards a translucent plastic receptacle about the size and shape of a car battery. He had other tubes extending from his arms too: insulin-drips and morphine-feeders, things like that. He looked like Caesar in the famous dream his wife Calpurnia describes: a perforated statue from which streams of bright-red life-blood gush forth, irrigating all of Rome; only the fluid flowing out of Petr's chest was pink—a lurid and synthetic pink that had an effervescent quality, like Cherryade. We chatted for a while, and as we did, whenever a part of him, a shoulder or a shin or a bit of chest, protruded from under the bedsheets, I would notice various smudgy, dark lumps pushing up beneath the skin. He had one just above his ankle; it was more than dark—it was black. The windows of the hospital were smudged and blackened too; his room was on the twenty-first floor and they obviously didn't bother to clean them that often, or at all. This upset me, much more than the fact of Petr's illness did. For crying out loud, I felt like shouting to the nurse, ward manager, whoever: if you can't save these people, at least clean the windows.

12.2 The next week brought a massive disappointment: I discovered that my parachutist theory didn't work. It was bogus; full of shit. The basic logistics of packing and storage, the security measures put in place to prevent tampering, and so forth—all this rendered it impossible. For example: divers, all divers, use only their own, personal packs, for which they are at all times responsible. They keep these in a special locker, to which they alone hold the key; when the packs are out of this, they never leave them unattended, never let them slip from their sight. I learned this from a piece of correspondence I'd started a month previously with a parachute-club safety officer. I read his email as I sat in the same spot in which I'd first made my "discovery," my dud one. The shock and disappointment I experienced as I read it were worse than those I would have had had the email told me my house and goods were all being confiscated, or that, as a result of some maternity-ward mix-up, I wasn't actually who I thought I was. It, too, was visceral; it made me feel first sick, then utterly depleted. After I'd read the email, I sat there for a long time, looking through the window. The sky, now, was grey and murky. It was cold. It was

only January, but the year already seemed jaded and old. I felt a
deep depression coming on.

12.3 Write Everything Down, said Malinowski. But the
thing is, now, it *is* all written down. There's hardly an instant
of our lives that isn't documented. Walk down any stretch of
street and you're being filmed by three cameras at once—and
even if you aren't, the phone you carry in your pocket pin-
points and logs your location at each given moment. Each
website that you visit, every click-through, every keystroke
is archived: even if you've hit *delete, wipe, empty trash,* it's still
lodged somewhere, in some fold or enclave, some occluded
avenue of circuitry. Nothing ever goes away. And as for the
structures of kinship, the networks of exchange within whose
web we're held, cradled, created—networks whose mapping
is the task, the very *raison d'être,* of someone like me: well,
those networks are being mapped, that task performed, by the
software that tabulates and cross-indexes what we buy with
who we know, and what they buy, or like, and with the other
objects that are bought or liked by others who we don't know
but with whom we cohabit a shared buying- or liking-pattern.
Pondering these facts, a new spectre, an even more grotesque
realization, presented itself to me: the truly terrifying thought
wasn't that the Great Report might be un-writable, but—quite
the opposite—that it had *already been written.* Not by a person,
nor even by some nefarious cabal, but simply by a neutral and
indifferent binary system that had given rise to itself, moved

by itself and would perpetuate itself: some auto-alphaing and auto-omegating script—that that's what it *was*. And that we, far from being its authors, or its operators, or even its slaves (for slaves are agents who can harbour hopes, however faint, that one day a Moses or a Spartacus will set them free), were no more than actions and commands within its key-chains. This Great Report, once it came into being, would, from that point onwards, have existed always, since time immemorial; and nothing else would really matter. But who could read it? From what angle, vantage-point or platform, accessed through what exit-jetty leading to what study (since all studies and all jetties were already written into it), could it be viewed, surveyed, interpreted? None, of course: none and no one. Only another piece of software could do that.

12.4 These ponderings had another consequence: around this time, my attitude not only to the Great Report but also towards Koob-Sassen underwent a sea-change. I started seeing the Project as nefarious. Sinister. Dangerous. In fact, downright evil. Worming its way into each corner of the citizenry's lives, re-setting ("re-configuring") the systems lying behind and bearing on virtually their every action and experience, and doing this without their even knowing it . . . I started picturing it, picturing its very letters (the *K* a body-outline, the *S*s folds of cloak, the hyphen a dagger hidden between these), slinking up staircases in the night while people slept, a silent assassin. That's how I started seeing it. I couldn't, at first, put my finger on a *particular* aspect or effect of it, nor on a specific instigator or beneficiary, that was itself inherently and unambiguously bad. But after a while I started telling myself that it was precisely this that made it evil: its very vagueness rendered it nefarious and sinister and dangerous. In not having a face, or even body, the Project garnered for itself enormous and far-reaching capabilities, while at the same time reducing its accountability—and vulnerability—to almost zero. What was to criticize, or to attack? There was no building, no Project Headquarters or Central Co-ordination Bureau. What person, then? The Minister with Shoes? She was no evil mastermind; she had no greater overview of the whole Project than I did. Her immediate boss, a man whose intellectual capacities (like all aristocrats, he was inbred) were held in almost open contempt by even his own cabinet members? The Project was supra-governmental, supra-national, supra-everything—and infra- too: *that*'s what made it so effective, and so deadly. I continued to ponder these things even as I laboured on, week-in, week-out, to help usher the Project into being, to help its first phase go live; and as I did, the more I pondered, ruminated, what you will, the more thoughts of this nature festered.

12.5 I started to reassess my own part in it all. I won't, as I've already stated, go into particulars; but suffice to say that my own role was tiny—tiny and lowly. I was, quite literally, underground: secreted down among Koob-Sassen's, as among the Company's, foundations, its underpinnings. This afforded me no power to shape the Project in a formal or official way—but to *un*-shape it, sabotage it even . . . That, I started whispering to myself, was another matter. Given license to burrow, could I not sniff out central axes and supports, and undermine them? Granted access to all areas, could I not lift a spanner from my tool-bag and, when no one else was looking, drop this in the engine rooms, jamming Project-cogs and Project-levers? Koob-Sassen may have been a giant reservoir into which flowed many tributaries—but I, being trusted to dip test-tubes into and take readings from any of these, was primed to slip out of my lab-coat's inner pocket a small phial, let trickle out of this a poison that, administered in even the minutest, most diluted form, could decimate whole populaces. Something as simple as providing faulty data, an intervention so mouse-like at point-of-entry, might engender, three or so steps down the chain, a sewer-monster of gargantuan proportions that, Godzilla-like, would rise up and smash everything; or issuing erroneous interpretations and assertions, or even insinuations, could lead to key decisions being made later that were catastrophically bad ones, circuits being wired and switches being thrown exactly the wrong way. I could do it, if I wanted: I could torch the fucker . . .

12.6 These fantasies grew on me. In my mind, I saw administrative buildings, bunkers, palaces come crashing down, heard glass splintering, stone tumbling, saw flames licking the skies: the Reichstag, Hindenburg, the falls of Troy and Rome, all rolled into one. And then my cohorts, that semi-occluded network of covert anthropologists I'd dreamed into being already: they could join me in the cause. Together, we could turn Present-Tense Anthropology™ into an armed resistance movement: I pictured them all scurrying around to my command, setting the charges, using their ethnographic skills to foment riots, to assemble lynch-mobs, to make urban space itself, its very fabric, rise up in revolt. I saw manholes erupting; cables spontaneously combusting; office wi-fi clouds crackling their way to audibility, causing hordes of schizoid bureaucrats, heads given over to cacophonies of voices, to flee their desks and tear about the streets, blood trickling from their ears . . . I had these visions as I sat down in my basement, rode the tube, or drifted off to sleep.

12.7 I visited Petr in hospital again. The worst thing about dying, he told me as I sat between his bed and the smudged windows, is that there's no one to tell about it. What do you mean? I asked. Well, he said, throughout my life I've always lived significant events in terms of how I'll tell people about them. What I mean is that even *during* these events I would be formulating, in my head, the way that I'd describe them later. Ah, I tried to tell him: that's a *buffering* probl . . . but Petr wasn't listening. The dying want to impart, not imbibe. When I was eighteen and I found myself in Berlin the day the Wall fell, he went on, as I watched the people streaming over, clambering up on it, hacking it down, I was rehearsing how to recount it all to friends after I got back home. *I watched the people sitting on the wall, chipping at it with their chisels, and the guards standing around not knowing what to do . . .* That's what I was thinking, he said, what was running through my head, right in the moment that I watched them chiseling and chipping. Same as when I saw the shootout in Amsterdam. What shootout? I said. Didn't I ever tell you about that? he asked. No, I answered. I found myself caught in the middle of a shootout between Russian gangsters as I came out of a restaurant, he explained. They were all firing from behind lamp-posts, dustbins, cars and so on, and I ducked into an alleyway and one of them was right there with me, holding this huge pistol, a gold one, which he balanced on the back of one hand as he shot it with the other. Wow, I said. Yes, Petr nodded—but the point is, that even as I cowered behind this gangster in this alleyway, I was practicing relating the episode when it was over. *He had a huge pistol—a gold one, no less! And he balanced it like this . . . and it recoiled like that . . .* Or: *I was just ten feet away from him . . . I thought that he might turn his gun on me, but he ignored me . . .* Trying out different ways of telling it, you see? Well, now, I'm about to undergo the mother, the big motherfucker, of all episodes— and I won't be able to dine out on it! Even if there turns out to be a Heaven or whatever, which there won't—but even if there does, I still won't be able to, since everyone else there will have lived through the same episode, i.e., dying, and they'll all go: *So what? That's boring. We know all that shit.* So it's lose-lose. Do you see my quandary? Yes, I said; I see that could be a problem.

12.8 The idea of Present-Tense Anthropology™ as armed struggle excited me. I thought of the seventies in Germany: the way those Baader-Meinhof people—highly educated, liberal-arts degrees in their back pockets—ran around causing mayhem. They wore such good clothes! Shirts with big, big collars; aviator sunglasses; flared cords. And they'd have sex with one another all the time: turn up at a safe-house in Munich, Düsseldorf, it didn't matter where, give the sign, show you're one of them, and *boom!* straight into bed. Same with the Patty Hearst gang in America: the funky heiress, honour-roll fine-art student, banging all those revolutionaries in her closet. I printed an image of her off the Internet and pinned it to my office wall. She wasn't actually that hot; it was the gun she held that made her sexy. I did the same with Ulrika Meinhof, who had a similar look about her: kind of plain and big-boned too. That didn't matter, though, I figured: *my* network of highly educated, highly trained subversives, armed with the very latest, anthropology-derived search-and-destroy techniques, would be the sexiest, best-dressed, most orgasmic revolutionaries ever.

12.9 One evening, I confided to Madison my dream of vandalizing everything, of using my insider status to wreak sabotage upon the Project. I knew a boy like you once, she said when I'd finished. Nobody had called me a *boy* in a long time. It was strange; I kind of liked it. But the thing is, she continued, turning from me in the bed, it won't be you doing the wreaking and the vandalizing. Oh? I said. Who *will* it be then? She turned half-back again, sat up, lit a cigarette and said: It isn't revolutionaries and terrorists who make nuclear power plants melt and blow their tops, or electricity grids crash, or automated trading systems go all higgledy-piggledy and write their billions down to pennies in ten minutes—they all do that on their own. You boys, she said, as once again I felt a double-pang of compliment and slight, are sweet. You all want to be the hero in the film who runs away in slo-mo from the villain's factory that he's just mined, throwing himself to the ground as it explodes. But the explosion's taking place already—it's always been taking place. You just didn't notice . . .

12.10 I sat facing her in silence. I didn't know what to reply. I tried to have sex with her again, but she wasn't interested; she just finished off her cigarette, scrunching its small stub onto a saucer lying beside the bed, then went to sleep. I lay awake for a long time, though, thinking about what she'd said. Lévi-Strauss claims that, for the isolated tribe with whom an anthropologist makes first contact—the tribe who, after being studied, will be decimated by diseases to which they've no resistance, then (if they've survived) converted to Christianity and, eventually, conscripted into semi-bonded labour by mining and logging companies—for them, civilization represents no less than a cataclysm. This cataclysm, he says, is the true face of our culture—the one that's turned away, from *us* at least. The order and harmony of the West, the laboratory in which structures of untold complexity are being cooked up, demand the emission of masses of noxious by-products. What the anthropologist encounters when he ventures beyond civilization's perimeter-fence is no more than its effluvia, its toxic fallout. The first thing we see as we travel round the world is our own filth, thrown into mankind's face.

12.11 That night, I eventually had a splendid dream. A rich and vivid one: one full of splendour. I was flying, like Daniel and Peyman in their helicopter, over a harbour by a city. It was a great, imperial city, the world's greatest—all of them, from all periods: Carthage, London, Alexandria, Vienna, Byzantium and New York, all superimposed on one another the way things are in dreams. We'd left the city and were flying above the harbour. This was full of bustle: tug-boats, steamers, yachts, you name it, bobbing and crisscrossing in water whose ridges and wave-troughs glinted in the sun, though it was nighttime. Out in the harbour—some way out, separated from the city by swathes of this choppy water—was an excrescence, a protuberance, a lump: an island. Was it man-made? Possibly. Its sides rose steeply from the sea; they were constructed of cement, or old bricks. The island was dark in hue; yet, like the sea, it seemed somehow lit up. As we approached it—flying quite low, parallel to the water—the buildings on it loomed larger and larger. These buildings—huge, derelict factories whose outer walls and rafters, barely intact, recalled the shells of bombed cathedrals—ran one into the next to form a single giant, half-ruined complex that covered the island's entire surface area. Inside this complex, rubbish was being burnt: it was a trash-incinerating plant. Giant mountains of the stuff were piled up in its great, empty halls, rising in places almost to where the ceiling would have been. They were being burnt slowly, from the inside, with a smouldering, rather than roaring, fire. Whence the glow: like embers when you poke them, the mounds' surfaces, where cracked or worn through by the heat, were oozing a vermilion shade of yellow. It was this glowing ooze, which hinted at a deeper, almost infinite reserve of yet-more-glowing ooze inside the trash-mountain's main body, that made the scene so rich and vivid, filled it with a splendour that was regal. Yes, *regal*—that was the strange thing: if the city was the capital, the seat of empire, then this island was the exact opposite, the inverse—the *other* place, the feeder, filterer, overflow-manager, the dirty, secreted-away appendix without which the body-proper couldn't function; yet it seemed, in its very degradation, more weirdly opulent than the capital it served. We were homing right in on it now: descending in our chopper through the factory-cathedral's shell, skimming the rubbish-piles as walls and rafters towered above us, gazing in awe and fascination at the glowing ooze, its colours as they morphed from vermilion yellow to mercurial silver, then on to purple, umber, burnt sienna, the foil-like flashing of its folds and gashes as light flowed across them. And, as we skimmed and veered and marvelled, a voice—the helicopter pilot's maybe, or some kind of commentator, or perhaps, as before with the roller-blader half-dream, just my own—announced, clearly and concisely: *Satin Island.*

12.12 I woke up. Madison was still asleep. It was just five o'clock. I pulled my clothes on and went home. Arriving there, I sat at my desk. Below me, on its surface, lay the wreckage of the Great Report's aborted launch. Outside, the day was, once more, grey. Small specks of water hung about the air. The courtyard, the pond, the concrete stepping-slabs set in it, the glass and concrete of the buildings all around, the general graphite texture of the dawn—these things seemed, in that moment, both consistent, all forming a single object with a single membrane, and, at the same time, porous, like some kind of wrapper that was starting to leak whatever content it was meant to keep wrapped up. Not fully awoken, still enfolded in my dream, I seemed to be consistent with this membrane too, to partake of its leakage. Leaning forwards with my forearm horizontal, perpendicular to the table, I used it to push a coffee cup and sundry other objects to one side. Then I wrote, with a pencil, directly on the blotter paper, on a small patch of it the forearm-pushing had exposed, the two words from my dream: *Satin Island.* Then I went and had a shower.

12.13 I couldn't shake the dream off all day: it sat right at the centre of my mind, consuming all my thoughts. Later, in the office, I took Patty and Ulrike down and pinned up in their place a bunch of images of barges carrying rubbish out to the Fresh Kills landfill site in New York Harbor. Staten Island: that's what that part of town was called—the fifth, forgotten borough, the great dump. That this place—both its name and function—had prompted my own dream seemed obvious: my sleeping mind had done little more than change *Staten* into *Satin*. I found the images online: pictures of barges, seagulls flocking around them, gorging themselves on their cargo; or of the garbage mountains photographed from above, from high up, even from beyond the stratosphere: like the Great Wall of China, the dump used to be visible from outer space. I say "used to be" because (as I found out) it had closed down in 2001, although it had briefly re-opened soon after to receive the rubble from the World Trade Center. Now, though, the miles of landfill were being transformed into nature parks. Beyond these, as before, stretched more miles of suburbia. All this the Internet told me. Next, I started following the trail of the word *satin*. Satin, as I knew from my old jeans-brief, is a type of weave, one in which warp yarns, floated over weft ones, form a glossy surface. I printed off an illustration showing the exact weave-structure. Then I looked at statins—a third term that, the more I reflected, was suggesting itself to me as a hidden link joining the actual word I'd heard, or maybe spoken, in my dream, *Satin,* and the un-enunciated but still obviously connoted *Staten*. Statins are cholesterol-lowering drugs inhibiting enzyme production in the liver. I found an illustration of their chemical composition, printed it off too, and pinned it next to the one showing satin's weave. I also printed off a picture showing wooden bleachers by an empty sports-field in the unincorporated town of Satin, Texas (population: 86); and the batting statistics of a former baseball player named Josh Satin, who had spent his career vacillating between major and minor leagues. Neither he nor the town could have been sources for my dream, since I'd not heard of either before; but I printed them off all the same, and plenty more besides. Soon all my walls were covered with such things.

12.14 Tapio phoned. Will you be here on Friday? he asked. Yes, I answered. Come see Peyman in the morning, he instructed me. Bring your Koob-Sassen dossiers. My Koob-Sassen . . . I repeated. The files, your findings, all the stuff you're working on, he said. I think I've circulated most of these already, I told him. This was true: I'd processed the civil-servant transcripts, the Parisian financial-service-worker ones and many other documents of that ilk—analyzed them, run them through the ethnographic mill, interpreted the data this procedure yielded and sent my interpretations up, through the relevant floors and across the requisite desks, to Peyman. Yes, said Tapio—but I mean the other stuff, the extra bits: that's what he wants to see. Oh, I said. I looked up at my walls. Whereas before, I'd been able to parlay my parachute wallpaper-fragments into a coherent and insightful contribution to the Company's overall work on Koob-Sassen (I'd since seen my in-transit metaphor, my perpetual-state-of-passage analogy, used in both internal and external Company memos on the subject), *these* images—the piles of rubbish, barges, seagulls—seemed to resist all incorporation into any useful or productive screed. I stared at the empty bleachers, trying to think of something to say. Eventually, Tapio broke the silence. Just bring up what you've got, he said. Okay, I answered; then he hung up.

12.15 The next—and final—time I visited Petr, I realized that I'd been wrong on the subject of the windows. They were still all smudged and blackened, as they had been last time—nothing had changed there. So was his flesh: the dark lumps were still pushing up from under the skin's surface, clouding it. My thinking on my first visit had been that, since the people in this ward, all facing imminent obliteration, had been positioned high up in this tall hospital, the conditions were perfect for affording them a really good sight of the world they would soon take their leave of, a bird's-eye view of one of its greatest and most teeming cities. Whether the placement had been done by design or chance, it was appropriate: if, as you die, you're meant to see your life, and life in general, with total clarity, then this small, parting 20/20 moment had been facilitated, laid on, set up by the architecture in which the patients found themselves—only to be confounded, snatched away again, by something as banal as a housekeeping oversight; or, if not an oversight, a small act of administrative penny-pinching. On this final visit, though, I came to see that, along the very lines that had made me view it as so wrong earlier, the windows' dirtiness was in fact totally correct. It was the world, its stuff, that had left its deposit—on the windows and in Petr's bones, his organs, flesh and arteries. The stuff of the world is black. If Petr's flesh was turning black it was because he'd let the world get right inside him, let it saturate him, until he was so full of it that it was bursting out again, erupting with a radiating luminescence. Thinking these thoughts while Petr talked to me of this and that (I have no recollection of what he spoke about that day), I began to suspect that he had already, in an almost literal sense, become an angel; looking around the ward, I grew convinced that it was also full of angels: figures whom the world had so deeply penetrated, flooded, impregnated that, refined in them, its forms and colours stripped down to their pure, constituent goo, it emanated back out from them—not as light but as its opposite: this formless, nameless blackness so dense and concentrated, so intense and blinding that, confronted by it, mortals like me had to shield our eyes.

12.16 I went straight home after this visit. My desk was as I'd left it, with those two words from my dream written in pencil on the one part of the blotter pad that wasn't cluttered up. Staring at them, I was struck by a thought: perhaps, I told myself, those words could form my Great Report. Not just its title, but its content too: the whole damn thing. Rather than hand Peyman new Koob-Sassen Project dossiers when I met him that Friday, I could announce that I'd completed this epochal task, and deliver it to him: all bound and laminated and what-have-you, with nothing but these two words in it. Perhaps, I told myself, I could present him with this actual blotter sheet. Framed? Folded? Scrumpled up? If scrumpled up, would it play out as a resignation notice? Probably. If framed, would he accept it, hang it on his office wall, sit looking at it as he talked, elaborated concepts and connected people, use it as a visual touch-point for all these activities? Possibly. Certainly, the fact that it came from me, and the context within which it was presented, would imbue it for him with all kinds of cryptic meaning. And besides, I felt with real conviction that it *was* full of this already: meaning of a genuinely deep and intense nature, whose sense eluded me but whose presence radiated, pouring into everything around it. Squinting, I tried to look at the blotter sheet as though it were a picture, rather than a page. The *S*s of both *Satin* and *Island* were sliced through by a thin, curving, brown line, since they lay on the circumference of a stain left by the coffee mug I'd cleared away. To the *d*'s right, slightly beneath it, like a comet's tail, was a big splodge of the same colour. Under this, in smaller letters, I wrote *Rumpelstiltskin. Secret name,* Peyman had said. I sat staring at the pad for a while longer; then, crossing out all of this last word's letters but the first *R,* I changed it to *Rosebud.*

12.17 Petr died two days later. I learned of his death by text. His wife, whom most of his friends didn't really know (they'd been estranged for several years), must, as his official next of kin, have been handed his mobile phone, and sent the announcement out to everybody in the contacts file—taxi firms and take-away restaurants and all. Petr passed away peacefully 11:25 a.m. today, it read. My first thoughts on receiving it—the thoughts you're meant to think in such a situation (*How sad; At least he's at rest; I'll miss him; And so forth*)—seemed so crass that I didn't even bother to think them. Instead, I thought about the message itself, its provenance. It had, as I said, come from Petr's estranged wife; but my phone, of course, like those of all the other people who would have received it, listed the sender as Petr. The network provider, logging every last transaction, would have marked the sender down as Petr too; if anybody cared to look it up in years to come, the record would affirm the same thing. To almost all intents and purposes, the sender *was* Petr. His existence, at that moment, was impressing itself on me, and on hundreds of others, with as much force as—if not more than—at any other time. All we need to do to guarantee indefinite existence for ourselves is to keep our network contracts running, and make sure a missive goes out every now and then. We could have factories of Chinese workers do it; pre-pay five or ten years by bequest-subscription; give them a bunch of messages to send out in rotation or on shuffle; or default to generic and random ones; I don't know. It would work, though. Key to immortality: text messaging.

12.18 On Friday I went up to Peyman's office. He was full of beans. The Project's first phase was about to go live. Everything was falling into place. I was holding a set of dossiers—physical, leather dossiers—beneath my arm, as per Tapio's instructions. None of them, to my knowledge, contained any type of data, code or misinformation whose effects would be subversive, let alone lethally destructive. So much for armed resistance. I was still nervous, though. But Peyman didn't ask me to show him anything. He just beamed at me, and told me that my contributions had been vital. He wanted me to go to New York the following month, to talk about it at a big symposium. That's funny, I said. What is? he asked. I've been thinking about New York Harbor for the last few days, I said. I should, of course, have handed him my blotter pad at this point—but I didn't have it with me, since that idea, plan, whatever, like the vandalism one and so many others, had fallen by the wayside. While Peyman talked, I tried to picture what it would have looked like on his wall: where it would have gone, how it would have changed that space's dynamic, coloured Peyman's, and the Company's, field of operations—perhaps coloured, by extension, our whole age. I let myself get lost in this imagining, and didn't take in what he was saying to me. After a while, I realized that he'd paused, and expected me to answer something. I tried to track my mind back a few seconds, to recover what he'd just been talking about; it was, I told myself, something to do with the statute of limitations. Maybe, Peyman was saying, you could use that as an analogy when you talk about our contribution to the Project? I suppose I could, I answered, adding something vague and non-committal about laws and terms of accountability viewed from an anthropological perspective.

Peyman seemed to approve. That sounds good, he said; go for it; and he called the meeting to a close. It wasn't until he sent me a follow-up email that I realized I'd misheard him, that it was the Statue of Liberty he'd actually been talking about.

12.19 Petr's funeral the following week was really weird. For a start, the funeral home was running behind schedule that day, so the previous service was still taking place when Petr's friends and family turned up. Parking was the main issue. All the spaces in the street around the home were taken by the vehicles of the mourners who were currently still burying their loved one. When these mourners finally filed out, their cortège still in loose formation, our group seemed unsure of what demeanour to adopt towards them. Some of us tried looking sad—which of course we were; but I mean that we tried to look sad for *them,* to show compassion for their loss. At the same time, we didn't want to intrude on their grief, so we tried to look neutral and indifferent as well. They, for their part, struck up a similarly mixed disposition towards us, with the result that the two groups, identically dressed, stood facing one another like a set of doubles. And our cars were double-parked as well: in collaboration with our unknown lookalikes, we had to manoeuvre these forwards and backwards to allow theirs out and ours in. Certain people took command, playing traffic cop, waving and shouting in a way that, given their attire, seemed ceremonial: suited officials, guiding boxes into holes.

12.20 But when the funeral proper started, it got even
weirder. Why? Because everything that was said about Petr
was wrong. I don't mean that it was wrongly nuanced or beside
the point or missing the essence of his character or anything
like that. I mean that it was simply, in a factual sense, false. For
a start, the service was a Christian one (Petr had been an athe-
ist); the minister described how Petr had found succour in his
faith during the months of his illness. He spoke of his family
life, and how his wife had been a rock of comfort and support
to him (they'd met from time to time, it's true; but they had,
as I mentioned, separated several years before his diagnosis).
It went on and on like this. The thought crossed my mind that
there had been a mix-up; that, due to that day's times being out
of kilter, we were listening to the spiel about the person whose
entourage we'd encountered on the way in, or perhaps the person after us, the one whose time-slot we'd slipped into. But
the minister called the man inside the coffin Petr; and he mentioned his job in IT, adding that his real passions were reserved
for certain leisure pursuits (windsurfing, chess) that I'd known
to hold no more than passing interest for him. As the litany of
falsehoods progressed, I thought about standing up, interrupting it and setting the record straight; the more it continued, the
more these thoughts took on a violent hue. I imagined striding
to the front, grabbing the minister by his frock, headbutting
him to the floor, jumping between the coffin and the furnace
and denouncing the entire procedure. Then we would all storm
the dais, tie the priest up, urinate onto his font, break Petr's

body out for a huge party that would bring the rafters down, and so on and so forth. Needless to say, we—I—didn't actually do any of these things. I just sat there, seething with quiet fury that this act of personal and cosmic fraudulence would never be requited.

13.

13.1 About three days after the funeral, I cornered Madison. Confronted her. Pinned her down. I *really* want to know what you were doing in Torino-Caselle, I said. We were in a restaurant. The starters had arrived. I'd ordered deep-fried squid; the tentacles, reprising a vague image from a previous reverie, reminded me of parachute cords, and hence of my now-defunct theory. I think it was the sense of impotence this brought about that spurred me into getting all aggressive on that other front. Madison was eating gravadlax. She paused in her chewing when I put the demand to her. The way I'd phrased it, my tone of voice, left no scope for dodging the question, brushing it away, like she had on at least two previous occasions. She finished her mouthful, laid her knife and fork down and said: I'd been in Genoa. What had you been doing there? I asked. Demonstrating, she said. Demonstrating what? I asked. No, demonstrating, she said, more emphatically. Protesting. Oh, I said; what against? The G8 summit, she said. In 2001, it was held in Genoa. I didn't know you were an activist, I said. Used to be, she corrected me; it was a long time ago.

I3.2 I pressed her further, of course. I felt that I was finally getting somewhere. She corrected herself a little now: it was really her boyfriend of the time who'd been the activist, she told me. He and his friends and associates, his general social circle, would descend on all these big G8 events. This time, they had converged from all around the world on Genoa. They'd stayed with scores of people, in a school building in the middle of the city, where the classrooms had been turned into dormitories, independent media centres and discussion rooms. It wasn't only protestors: there were journalists and academics too, she said. The gathering had the air of a big carnival, a circus of ideas. Sounds fun, I said. It was, she said, until the police arrived. They kicked down the school's doors in the small hours of the morning, when everyone was asleep, rushed up into the dorms and started attacking people in their beds. Shit, I said. Yes, she answered. As soon as people on the top floor realized what was going on, we ran out to the fire escapes—but police were waiting on these too. The raid was well-planned. So what did you do? I asked. We held our hands up and surrendered, she said. But that didn't matter: they attacked us too. They stamped on people's legs, and heads, and chests; I saw this one guy's chest crumple as they stamped on it—and heard his ribs cracking too. It's a strange sound, she told me; a bit like those old chocolate bars—the ones with the synthetic honeycomb inside, that used to crunch when you bit into them. Crunchies? I asked. Yes, she answered, that's right: Crunchies. Those were good, I said. Yes, she concurred; I'm not sure you can get them anymore.

13.3 Why have I never heard about this episode? I asked. I've never spoken about it before, she said. No, I said, I mean why didn't I read about it in the press—especially if there were journalists there, staying in the very building where it happened? U., she said, this took place in the late summer of 2001, just before September the eleventh. After that, all other news was blown out of the water: no one was interested in what had gone on in Genoa, or anywhere else. It was as though it had never taken place. She paused, while our main course was laid in front of us. I'd ordered pork; she'd chosen chicken, I think—either that or duck. We sat in silence for a few seconds after the waitress had left, tasting our food. Then Madison picked up where she'd left off. Sometimes, she said, I even wonder if it actually took place myself. Are you still in touch with people from that time? I asked. My boyfriend's circle, you mean? she asked back. I nodded. No, she said: I don't have any contact with them. And besides, I don't think they're a circle anymore.

13.4 The Project's first phase had gone live: it was up and running, rolled out, operational, whatever. Its implementation had been deemed a great success. By whom? I don't know. Deemers. And the Company's contribution had been praised, by praisers, as quite brilliant. And my own input into this had been held up and singled out, by Peyman himself, as particularly productive. All this was going to my head. I even glanced about the restaurant, to see if anybody recognized me. This was ridiculous, of course: the people there had probably never even heard about Koob-Sassen, let alone my role in it. And this, perhaps, was not a bad thing, after all: the thwarted saboteurs that I myself had mobilized then turned my back on, the hit squads of vengeful revolutionaries, wouldn't know who to shoot when they came looking for the traitor.

13.5 Did you get stamped on? I asked Madison. I got pushed down the fire escape, she said. I bruised myself, but it wasn't that bad. And that was it? I asked. Did the police leave after that? Madison laughed into her food: a sudden, short laugh that was like a cough. No, U., she said; that wasn't it at all. That was just the beginning. So what happened next? I asked. The police rounded us up, she said. They got us all into a courtyard, about a hundred people, and they hemmed us in and formed a human square around us, two or more thick, and took it in turns to wade in to the middle of this square and club people and stamp on them some more. Then they made us walk out to these trucks that were parked just outside. Hadn't you heard them pulling up? I asked. No, she replied. They put us in these trucks, and drove us to a police station. They unloaded us into some other courtyard there, where there were lots more police, fresh ones, all fired up and ready to let loose. Which is exactly what they did: they clubbed and stamped on people to their hearts' content. And all the time, more and more captured demonstrators were arriving: people I didn't recognize, who'd been staying in other places—hostels, houses, student dormitories. Truck after truck would pull up, and these people, all bruised and bloodied just like us, would be led out of them, and fed into the middle of this square whose sides were made of policemen, and then beaten up some more.

13.6 How long did this go on for? I asked her. It's hard to tell, said Madison. Perhaps an hour. When new people stopped arriving and the ones already there couldn't stand up to be beaten anymore, or didn't even react much when they were kicked and stamped on, the police eased off a bit. New officers came out of the main station holding sheets of paper, instructions or something, and after consulting these for a while, they started organizing all the people in the courtyard into groups. I don't know what the logic of it was: it's not as though they just divvied the crowd up into blocks where we were standing. Instead, they'd make five of us go and stand in one corner of the courtyard, then bring two more people over from some other part, and two more from a third, and make us stand in rows of three, like soldiers—three rows of three, so there were nine in every group. Then they might move four people out of one group and make them join another group in the far corner while they brought in three from yet another group and one more from another still to bring the number up to nine again. Whatever rationale was behind it, they carried out this sorting quite assiduously, for a long time. Then, eventually, one by one, the groups were marched into the station building itself.

13.7 Our plates, largely untouched, were lying in front of us. The waitress had skirted by a couple of times, to see if everything was all right. It was a good restaurant. Most other diners were on their dessert course, or their coffee. The ones paying their bills and leaving weren't being replaced by others; it was well into mid-afternoon. What happened when you came inside the building? I asked Madison. Well, she said, everyone was singing. Singing? I repeated. Yes, she said. The police were singing? I asked. No, she said; mainly the demonstrators. Protest songs, you mean? I asked. God no, she answered: they were singing songs the police were making them sing. Someone in Madison's group, an Italian guy, had whispered to her that they were fascist songs, from Mussolini's time. The cops had been leading the singing, moving their batons like conductors do. If anybody didn't sing, Madison explained, or didn't sing loud enough, the police would jerk the batons' ends into their midriffs, upwards, from below—which would knock the wind out of them, of course, but then they had to sing immediately afterwards, wind or no wind, or they'd get another jerk. What if you didn't know the words? I asked. They taught us the words, she answered—like in nursery school: it was a singalong. While it went on, they carried on dividing up the groups: breaking them down into smaller groups of about five people, then separating these out into clusters of two or three. We had to sing while they were doing this to us, she said. It was so strange. Eventually, I found myself with just one other woman. She was German, I think. She couldn't really say much since her jaw had been all smashed up. And besides, we couldn't talk: we had to keep on singing—singing Italian words. This woman couldn't do this very well, of course; but since the cops would baton-jerk her if she stopped, she forced the words out somehow, without really shaping them properly in her mouth. I got the sense that she was German all the same, said Madison, just from the way the sound came from her throat.

13.8 She paused, and took a big bite of her duck or chicken. I watched her mouth chewing. Then I looked down at my plate, and pushed a vegetable around for a few seconds. After a while I asked: What happened next? Well, Madison continued, this girl and I were taken through a door, and down a corridor, and down a set of stairs and up another one, and down another corridor, then through a final door that led out to a car park. We were taken to this car, she said—an unmarked one. There were two guys in the front, in plain clothes; and the guy in the passenger seat turned round and stared at us both for a while, looking us up and down; then he pointed to the other girl and said something in Italian to the uniformed cops who'd brought us there, and they removed her from the car again.

13.9 And you? I asked. Me they drove off, she said. It was dawn, and we were driving through the streets—but the guy in the passenger seat told me not to look outside. I understood he meant that, since he kind of barked the same instruction at me every time I turned my head to one side or the other. So I just looked forwards, at his seat's back. These plain-clothes guys drove me around for a long time, she went on; when they eventually stopped, I looked out, finally, and saw another courtyard—a cobbled one, with some kind of villa curving and jutting all around it. The villa was pretty, she said: an old house of several floors, with ivy climbing up the walls and wooden shutters on the windows. They brought me from the car, and led me to this villa. Inside, it was like a big family house—either that, or some kind of institution. There was a big reception area with a marble floor; and there was a desk here, with a reception-ist behind it. The plain-clothes policeman, the passenger-seat guy, told me to empty out my pockets, and he put my keys and passport and whatever else I had there in a tray that the recep-tionist slid onto a shelf behind her. Receptionist? I said. You're checking into a hotel now? That's the thing, said Madison: it didn't feel like another police station. It wasn't a police sta-tion. I don't know what it was. This receptionist was perfectly polite—not friendly exactly, but courteous. Even the plain-clothes passenger-seat guy wasn't barking at me anymore. The lady handed him a receipt for my things; then he escorted me across the marble floor, and gestured, with politeness also, for me to go through a wooden door with stained-glass panels in it, that he held open for me. And we walked down another long corridor, and down some steps again, until, eventually, we came to a plain white door, which he knocked on quietly. A voice answered; my guy opened the door and, standing back once more, ushered me in.

13.10 She paused again. Well, what was in the room? I asked her. A man, she said. A man? I repeated. Yes, she said. What kind of man? I asked. I don't know, she said: a man. How old was he? I asked. About sixty, she said. What did he look like? I asked. He was smartly dressed, she said; quite portly; he had grey hair that was turning white, combed neatly back. He was sitting in a red leather armchair in the middle of this room. He asked my escort something, and my escort answered very deferentially; then he dismissed the escort with a wave, and we two were alone. What type of room was it? I asked. I couldn't really say, said Madison; it looked a little like a doctor's room or a laboratory. There was this strange contraption at the far end, past the armchair: it was like a chair as well, but with appendages and segments that looked as though they could be manipulated and adjusted—kind of like a dentist's chair, an old one. Everything in the room was old; I don't know why I said it looked like a laboratory. Maybe I meant an old laboratory, where you'd see thick jars of chemicals lining the shelves. But there were no chemicals, and no shelves. There was a small window. A few feet from this there was a drape that hung along the wall: this big, wrinkled curtain. I don't know why it was there—maybe for warmth; behind it there was just a wall, as far as I could tell. But the curtain gave the room the look of a theatre, or an auditorium—or maybe a recording studio, with the drape there for muffling. The place seemed pretty quiet and isolated: there was no background noise or anything like that. Apart from, Madison continued, that there was this kind of gizmo on a table not far from this man's red chair. What do you mean, a gizmo? I asked. A *thing,* she said. A piece of electronic hardware. Maybe a receiver, a detector, wavelength modulator, I don't know. It was old too: the kind of thing they'd have used twenty years ago, perhaps more. It made an electronic noise. When I came in, said Madison, this man was fiddling with this thing, as though he were tuning it.

13.11 She picked a caper from her plate. Then what happened? I asked. Madison held the caper up, as though inspecting it, then set it down on her plate's side. Eventually, she said, the smartly dressed man in the room turned round to face me. He beckoned me over and told me to turn around in front of him: revolve, rotate. I had a scrape on my neck, which he looked at closely, holding my hair back. He asked me, in English, where else I'd been injured, so I told him: *Here, above the hips; and here, just on the elbow* (Madison pointed to these spots now, in the restaurant, as though I were this man)—and I thought for a moment that he was a doctor. Or maybe a lawyer, with his expensive suit. But he wasn't. He reached down behind the red armchair and picked up, first, a black wand. A wand? I repeated. Yes, she said: a plasticky-metallic kind of pointer. Then, she carried on, a glove—a thick one, like a gardening- or oven-glove. He slipped the glove onto his right hand; and, holding the wand in this, he touched the thin end to my midriff. Then the glove twitched, and I felt a huge electric surge run through me. What the fuck? I said to Madison. It was a cattle-prod I guess, she told me. Did it hurt? I asked her. Yes, U., she replied, it hurt. It hurt more than anything I've ever felt before or since. But it was over very quickly; and I was too startled to shout or scream or anything. After he'd zapped me with his prod, this man just stood beside me, calmly, seeing what I would do. What did you do? I asked her. Nothing, she answered. I just stood there. Where would I have gone? He watched me while I stood there. He still had the prod, down by his side. I somehow knew, though, that he wasn't going to keep on zapping me: he just wanted me to know that he *could*, if he wanted to—and wanted me to show him that I understood that. Which I did, by standing still. Once this understanding had been reached, we could begin.

13.12 Begin? I asked her. Begin what? What we did for the next couple of hours, said Madison, is that he made me strike up and hold certain postures. Postures? I asked. Postures, she repeated; like a fashion shoot. I had to turn one way, then another, then to bend, then hold my arms up, stick my leg out, things like that. This man told me exactly what to do; he was really precise. From time to time, if I didn't have the posture quite right, he would raise the prod, to threaten me; once, when I let my arms fall to my side since I was too tired to keep them raised like he'd instructed me, he zapped me again; after that I kept them up, tired or not. And all the while, while forcing me into these shapes, he was consulting with and nudging at this other thing. What other thing? I asked. The gizmo-thing, she said; this modulator or detector. It had a small screen on it, that had lines running across it: wave-lines, like you might get on earthquake-predicting machines, or on those other ones that show stock-market prices as they fluctuate. He'd look at the screen, then look at me, and make me shift my arm an inch this way or that way, or rotate my head clockwise a tiny bit, or anti-clockwise, or tell me to jut my chin or chest out; then he'd look back at the thing, and turn a knob a little bit, and say something to himself, or to the machine, or to whoever was behind it, on the other end. The other end? I asked. It was a two-way appa-ratus? It seemed that way, she said; I thought that it might be a radio, some kind of intercom or clunky, antique walkie-talkie. But then there were no voices coming out of it, at least not at his end: just electronic whining, crackling, things like that. He listened to it, though, really attentively, and watched the mod-ulating wave as if its jags and vacillations *meant* something. I think that he was being sent instructions through this thing. Instructions? I repeated. Yes, she said. By whom? I asked. I don't know, she said. That's the thing. This man was obviously important. I could tell that just by looking at him, from his clothes and his demeanour, from the way my plain-clothes guy deferred to him, from the house and its whole rigmarole: everything seemed to orbit around him and this room. Not just the house, but *everything:* the raid on the school, the beatings, the weird sorting and dividing in the courtyard, all that stuff— this man, somehow, seemed *behind* all that. And at the same time, he himself seemed to be governed by these messages crackling and zig-zagging their way to him from . . . I don't know: from somewhere else. I said there were no voices in the noise, she went on; but actually, after a while, I started hearing, at a certain point within the crackling, something that sounded a little bit like children's voices. Children's voices? I repeated. Yes, she said. They'd kind of separate out from the general sound, like strands that had come loose, then merge and fluff back into it again. What were they saying? I asked her. Nothing, she replied; at least not anything that sounded like real words, in Italian or any other language; just shouts and chirps and little bits of sing-song—general infant babble. It was very indistinct: as soon as I thought I'd picked these voices out and tuned into them properly, they'd disappear again.

13.13 These postures that he made you strike up, I asked Madison: were they erotic? Some of them were, she said. Sometimes I had to bend over and stick my arse up in the air, or pull up my culottes and show my thigh, or slip my shirt down off my shoulder. But all this was pretty mild; I mean, he could have made me strip, or raped me, or done anything at all, given the situation. The positions he was making me assume were more like the postures of classical statues, or old paintings. He was getting off on it, though, kind of: I could hear his breathing growing heavier, and hear these quiet grunts, these moans, coming from deep inside his chest. But these were beyond sexual. If they *were* sexual, the excitement wasn't exactly for *me,* but for some kind of relation between me, the angles of my limbs and torso, and the machine, the rhythms of its crackles, beeps and oscillations. When these fell into alignment, when we got it *right*—well, then he'd moan more deeply, with real pleasure. After a while, I came to recognize these rhythms. What do you mean? I asked. There were these sequences of pitch and frequency, she said, that faded into one another and then came back round again, only a little differently each time. It got so I could recognize these sequences, and know which part of them we were in at a given moment, and what I should be doing at this part, and what was coming next. I came to know just what it was he wanted, how I had to move; he didn't need to keep telling me what to do. This made him really satisfied. More than just satisfied, she said: it seemed to move him deeply.

13.14 Madison looked round the restaurant. The place had emptied out now. The waitresses were sitting at a table, wrapping newly washed cutlery in napkins, which they folded with a regular and automated movement. Two chefs were sitting at another, going through a list of stocks, ingredients, supplies. No one was pushing us to leave; they appeared to have forgotten us, just as we'd forgotten both them and the food they'd made us. So you struck these postures, I said. You ran through sequences of them, and this man watched you. Yes, she answered. He and I kept this up for an eternity. Time seemed to have stopped. We could have been the only people in the world—the first-ever people, a new Eve and Adam. Time seemed, she said again, to have just . . . stopped: to be suspended, while we two performed this strange ballet being choreographed from elsewhere. You mean *you* did, I said. No, said Madison: we both did. He was moving too. At first he moved his body and his limbs to show me how I had to move mine; then, as I learnt the sequences, his own movements grew less emphatic, and then almost imperceptible. But they were still going on: his leg would buckle and his knee extend a little; his right shoulder would angle upwards, and his left arm twitch below the elbow. He was as much a part of the choreography as I was. After a while, he closed his eyes; and yet his limbs still subtly moved and twitched and angled, to the same rhythm, the same pattern, to the modulating sound of the machine and my own corresponding sequences of postures. He was, like I said, deeply moved. At one point I saw big tears rolling down his cheeks. You saw . . . ? I started asking, but she went straight on, cutting me off. Then these gave over to sobs, she said. *Sobs?* I asked. That's right, Madison answered: he was sobbing. He was a big man, as I mentioned: portly. The sobbing shook his frame. His face had deep, grey wrinkles cut into its cheeks; the tears ran into these, and ran out through them; they were like drainage conduits. Eventually he sat down in the leather chair, slumped deep into it and gave me to understand that the spectacle, charade, the game, was over: I could stand down. And at this moment, the machine's pitch slackened too: its jags and crackles, that had been so charged and jumping, went all elongated, flattened, like the thing was running down. Apart from the bit that sounded like children's voices, she said—that part of it remained, and seemed to become clearer . . .

13.15 She paused, and held her head alert, as though she were still hearing, in the restaurant, these children's voices. So what did you do? I asked her. I stood down, she said. I mean, I stopped making the movements, stopped striking up and running through the postures, and just stood in front of him. After a while, when his sobbing had subsided, he opened his eyes and looked at me. He still had the wand in his hand, hanging by the chair's side; and he passed this to me now. Passed it to *you*? I asked. Yes, Madison replied: he handed me the wand, the cattle-prod. What did you do with it? I asked. I took it from him, she said, and set it down on the floor some feet away. Then I turned back to face him, to see what he wanted; but his face had gone all vacant. So I moved over to the window. When I looked out of this, I saw a garden, running away beneath it. The villa was built on a hill: although we'd gone down one floor from the entrance to get to this room, on the side that I was looking out of now, the far side, the room was two floors above ground level. There was this garden, and there were two children playing in it. They can't have been much more than five years old. It was their voices I'd been hearing, coming through the window—not through the machine; I'd just assumed that, because the voices had been caught up in the machine's general noise. Now that this had dwindled to a slow, quiet croak, they carried to me clearly. The children were playing tag or something; sudden shrieks of laughter and excitement leapt from them and ricocheted around the room. I moved a little to the side and lifted the drape, this crinkled curtain. Behind it there was just more wall, as I'd thought. Then I turned back to face the room's interior. I went up to the chair with segments and appendages, the maybe-dentist's chair. It had these straps on it, restraining straps I guess; but these were loose, unbuckled and all worn. Then I inspected the machine, she said: the gizmo, this big, clunky apparatus that had held both me and this man in its power for so long. It really was old: it had all these ancient valves and needles set in a worn metallic frame, and knobs with faded numbers round their circumference. The screen was gridded; the speaker's grille was cross-hatched, set on a diagonal. Nothing was really coming out of the speaker any-more, though—just a kind of sonic dribble. The wave-lines on the screen were still there; but they were placid and immo-bile. Whatever this thing had been doing, it wasn't doing it anymore. It had gone all vacant too, just like its operator . . . Madison seemed to go vacant at this point herself, staring ahead into the restaurant's dead space. So what did you do? I asked her. I sat down beside him, she said, on the floor, leaning against the armchair's side. His hand was hanging limp beside my shoulder. I just sat there, and he sat there too, and all the objects in the room just sat there, doing nothing, for a long, long time.

13.16 We sat there too, in silence, Madison and I, in this restaurant. I couldn't think of anything to say. In the fading afternoon light, waitresses and chefs were eating now, taking late lunch or early supper. Eventually I asked her: How did you get out? Out of where? she asked back. The room, I said:

how did you leave the room? I didn't, she said. Not at first. I fell asleep against his chair. I must have been awake for two whole days by this point, if you don't count the hour of sleep I'd had back at the school building, before the raid. I was really tired. Did he sleep too? I asked. Who? she asked. The man, I said. Maybe, she said. He sat in the armchair for a long time without moving. His breathing was regular and deep, and so was mine; and then I was asleep. When I woke up, he was gone. The machine had been switched off: no more wave-lines, even flat ones; no more noise at all. And the children's voices had disappeared too. Just moments after I woke up, another man walked in; perhaps his footsteps coming down the corridor, approaching, were what woke me. This new man was much younger—in his thirties, maybe. He was smartly dressed as well, but his clothes weren't expensive like the older one's. This man was friendly: he asked me if I'd rested; and I told him yes, I had; and he said: *Well, we'd better get you on your way.* He spoke to you in English? I asked Madison. Yes, she replied; good English, with a slight Italian accent. I thought he might have been a consular official—a junior one. They use locals for that, don't they? she asked. I don't know, I said; is that what he turned out to be? Who? she asked. This other man, I said. I don't know, she replied; I never found out. I mean, I never asked. He led me from the room, and through some other corridors and doors, not the ones I'd first come through, and then down some other steps; and suddenly I found myself back in the lobby, the reception. You mean *up* some steps, I corrected her. No, she insisted: down. This man, she went on, handed my receipt, which he must have been given by the plain-clothes guy, to the receptionist, and I got all my stuff back. And he said: *There: all accounted for?*—something like that. And I told him: *Yes, I think so,* or something. I didn't have my mobile, but that had been left behind at the school. He led me back out through the front door, to the cobbled courtyard; and he said, still in a friendly, helpful voice, that I shouldn't go back to the centre of town, since police were still rounding up people who looked like protestors. *Go this way,* he said as we got to the road, pointing to the right; then he turned round and went back to the villa.

13.17 And you? I asked. Me? she asked back. Yes, I answered: what did you do? I walked in the direction he'd suggested, she said. I'd come out into some kind of suburb. It was a nice day: warm and sunny, languid. I remember there were flowers along the roadside, hanging over garden walls. I passed some kind of workshop, where a man was cutting something with a saw; then shops. There was this clothing shop. I went inside and bought some new clothes with my credit card: a shawl, a hat, a skirt. They weren't particularly good clothes; just the kind of things that middle-aged, suburban women wear. And while I was in the shop, I tried to ask if there was a bus stop or metro station somewhere nearby; and the shop-woman told me *ferrovia*—railway—and, sure enough, there was a train station just a hundred yards away. One platform took you back to the centre of town; the other one led to Turin. So I took the next train from the second one. And on the train, on a route map in

the corridor, I saw a little airport-icon by the stop just before
Turin, with *Internazionale* written next to it; so that's where I
got off, and bought a ticket back to London—again, with my
credit card. I remember thinking that it was ironic. What was?
I asked. That it was my credit card that saved me after I'd been
protesting against capitalism, she said. Oh, I see, I told her; I
suppose it was. There was a plane leaving in about five hours'
time, she carried on. I bought a ticket, and sat there for the
next five hours, hardly moving, waiting for the plane. And that,
Madison concluded, laying her hands, palms-down, across the
tabletop and looking at me with a frank but empty gaze, is how
I came to be in Torino-Caselle Airport.

13.18 By now, the staff had finished eating. Dusk was coming down, but they hadn't switched on the restaurant's lighting
yet. Madison sat back in her chair. As her face retreated from
me, it grew indistinct. The thing about Turin, she said after a
pause, is that it's where . . . I know, I said: it's where the shroud
is from. No, Madison told me; I wasn't thinking of that. I was
thinking of that other guy, who went mad. What other guy? I
asked. The famous philosopher, she answered. Kierkegaard
or Schopenhauer or someone; the one who said that God was
dead. Oh, I told her: you mean Nietzsche. Maybe, she said.
I'm pretty sure it was Nietzsche, I said. Whoever, she replied;
it doesn't matter: the point is—I found this out later—he saw
a horse being beaten in a square in Turin, and he lost it. Can
you imagine? After all the questions that he must have grap-

pled with, the complex, universal stuff he'd thought and written about, it was a horse that did his mind in: a dumb horse. Its owner, driver, operator or whatever, she continued, was whipping it; and Kierkegaard or Nietzsche or whoever saw this act of cruelty, and it wacked him out, sent him insane. He never wrote another book. For the first time in the conversation, she looked genuinely disturbed. Of all things, she said: a *horse* . . . Her voice had gone all faint. So had her face: darkness was gathering around it, smudging its parameters more and more with each passing minute. We sat in silence for a while, listening to the muffled noise of traffic and the low-level bustle of the staff as they readied the place for the evening sitting.

14.

14.1 The following week, I flew off to New York, and this symposium. I didn't have to give a presentation or a lecture or anything like that—just sit on a bunch of panel discussions. To my surprise, I found myself (in stark contrast to Frankfurt) being fêted at every turn. Peyman had clearly put the word out. Despite saying almost nothing in any of these conversations, I was accorded almost sycophantic reverence, simply for being (as it was stated time and again) one of the Koob-Sassen Project's "architects" or "engineers." Any protest I made about the grotesque exaggeration contained in this label, any confession of my utterly diminutive contribution to the whole thing, of how my little subterranean scratching-around had formed a tiny piece of a huge jigsaw, and so on—all these were written down to some notion of quaint British modesty, and had the opposite effect to that intended, boosting my presumed rank and prestige even more. The trade press were all over the event; after each panel, there'd be short interviews, at which off-the-cuff utterances, none of which I can remember, were extracted from me; then I and the other panelists would be ushered to limousines and whisked off to meals in restaurants so expensive that they didn't print the prices on the menus; not that we were paying.

14.2 On the third day of this, several hours before I was due to fly back out of JFK, I managed to extricate myself from this circus. I thus found myself with a fair stretch of time, free time, and no desire to fill it up with anything. I rode the subway for an hour or so, getting off here and there, walking a few blocks, then burrowing back down into the next lettered stairwell that I came across. I followed no route in particular—just crossed and crisscrossed, switched back, re-traversed the same stretches of track; but all the same, I found myself being drawn, like some weak dowser's rod, lower and lower downtown. Eventually, abandoning the illusion that this descent was taking place by chance rather than design, I took the decision to do what I'd already been doing half-intentionally: that is, to travel right down to Manhattan's very base, and to the ferry terminal perched on its southernmost tip.

14.3 South Ferry is the subway station serving the terminal itself; but for some reason it was closed, so I got off at Rector Street instead. A sign at one end of the platform directed passengers towards the 9/11 Memorial; another, at the far end, read *Ferries to Staten Island*. It was odd to see those last two words printed out, in public, big and bold and official, after having stared at them, or their variants, in private for so long—as though I were now physically moving through one of my own dossiers: past its coordinates, along its arbitrary channels of association. Beyond the sign, a narrow staircase carried me up to a street bathed in late-winter sunlight. Old buildings bordered this. One of them had its name emblazoned above its portico: New York State Department of Motor Vehicles. Others, untitled, had the look of civic buildings too: tax offices, perhaps, or public records depots. Above these buildings, dwarfing them, the half-completed Freedom Tower's crane-studded skeleton rose up. The thrum of sightseeing helicopters hung about the air; behind the Motor Vehicle building I could see one taking off, its glass nose sniffing the ground to which it glided parallel for a few metres before peeling away laterally skywards; another hovered, its head angled more aloofly upwards as it waited to land. The intermittent *beep-beep-beep* of reversing buses broke up the chopper blades' deep, gut-vibrating frequencies, or at least punctuated them. Buses were everywhere: MTA buses turning around or idling at their downtown end-point; tour buses disgorging tourists or awaiting new ones. Men in yellow jackets hawked tickets for these buses, for the helicopters and for boats: aerial and ground tours of Manhattan, cruises to Ellis and Liberty Islands. No one, of course, was selling tours to Staten Island, since the crossing was free—and, even if it hadn't been, no tourist would have wanted to go there.

14.4 I wanted to go there. Why? I don't know. Why does anyone do anything? I was, as I'd anticipated I would be, depressed. I'd been this way for months. Despite the Project's evident, or apparent, success; despite my own "pivotal" role in the Company's contribution to this monumental undertaking, all the plaudits it was winning me (there'd doubtless be a raise, an elevated status in the Company, perhaps even a high-up, or at least above-ground, office—how I'd miss the sound of ventilation!)—none of this meant anything to me. Nothing meant anything to me. Present-Tense Anthropology™? The Parachutist Mystery? Trashed, pulverised, dissolved back into the whimsy-froth from which they'd bubbled up. The Torino-Caselle Enigma? Madison's story was, like Lévi-Strauss's tribe, just fucking weird. What dot-codex could be salvaged from that? And yet the rich and vivid island-dream had stayed with me, cached itself somewhere deep inside, and was now growing, pulsing as it rose back to the surface, radiating with a prospect, with an overwhelming promise, of significance. Something, I told myself with an assurance that I can't explain, nor could I then, but which all the same, perhaps for that very reason, seemed completely watertight—something would happen if I went to Staten Island. I didn't know what; but something would. And something would make sense—if not the whole caboodle, at least *something*. Something is not nothing, even if it isn't everything. Like a shipwrecked sailor clinging to a piece of driftwood, or a gambler down to his last chip reaching for the dice to take one final roll, I'd gravitated down here, to the bottom of Manhattan, armed with nothing more than an idea of getting on this ferry. Would I come back on it again? Perhaps; perhaps not. Anything seemed possible.

14.5 Skirting the edge of Battery Park, I managed to pick out a couple of small signs for the ferry terminal: cheaply printed ones, clamped onto lamp-posts, jostling for space with better, more official signs pointing to Battery Park, to Bowling Green, or to a second Memorial, this one for veterans of Vietnam. I had to weave and thread my way through queues, lines, gaggles, general throngs of people speaking Spanish, Japanese, French, German, Mandarin and who knows what else, before, behind a broken veil of pretzel stands and gyros trucks, the terminal loomed into view. The building itself looked new: all glass and metal, not unlike the Company's headquarters, with giant, steel-cast, three-dimensional letters mounted above the entrance, boldly announcing *STATEN ISLAND FERRY*. As I followed the path round towards the building, more food stands and lamp-posts, passing through my field of vision, temporarily erased some of these letters, so the sign read SATE I LAND, then, a few seconds later, STATE IS ERR. This intrigued me; I started moving back and forth erratically to tease new couplings out by eliding some letters, restoring others. I got SAT AND FRY, SANS LAND, TEN SANDER, TEN IS LAND . . . The letters were like Scrabble pieces rearranging themselves in an attempt to form a legitimate word; or like the numbers on a combination lock, revolving singularly and in series through their permutations, each *click* bringing with it the chance that the correct sequence, the *true* number, will eventually reveal itself, crack open whatever safe it's protecting, spill its contents. FER. AIL. END. S A I L— then, to my great excitement, on the fourth or fifth pass down the same ten-yard stretch, S AT I N. An irrational elation overtook me as this last word spelled itself out. It was short-lived, though: soon the word morphed into STA I N; then the roof's overhang eclipsed all but the first two letters: ST. Coincidentally, at the same moment I became aware of a man's voice off to my left pronouncing, over and over, a word that sounded like a contraction of *Starbucks: Stix* or *Stycks*. He said it in an interrogatory manner. Turning round to where the voice was coming from, I saw that its owner was an old-style confectionary vendor selling candy-floss out of a street-cart. He was asking two kids whose dad was buying them some whether they wanted it in a bag or on (and this, of course, was the word I was mishearing) sticks. The kids chose sticks. After he'd handed them the billowing, synthetic stuff, they stood munching it silently, staring back at me with hostile, sticky faces.

14.6 The terminal's interior, despite its new façade, was dingy. Parts of it were boarded up, awaiting repair. The smell of popcorn, hot dogs, pizza and donuts hung about the concourse, impregnating air that was much warmer than the air outside—cloying and heavy, too. People were milling about, waiting for the ferry: normal, everyday folk who commuted on it daily. A few of them wore suits—cheap, polyester ones, the standard-issue outfit of the low-white-collar ranks; but most wore plain, casual clothes. They looked bored, frumpy, tired, unhealthy, overweight and generally just very, very *normal*. An MTA man armed with a megaphone was telling them that the 3:30 boat would be arriving *momentarily*. He actually meant "in a moment"; but the term's correct sense, *for* a moment, given these ferries' quick and constant turnaround, was carried over in his misuse of it. The man's megaphone, and his impatient and authoritarian tone, gave the scene the air of an evacuation: looking at the drab, deflated passengers, I pictured refugees being herded off towards some makeshift temporary shelter. One of them was hobbling on crutches; another had a cane; a third one a badly fitting wig. The walls of the terminal were largely bare. On one side of the sliding doors towards which these walls funneled the passengers, there was a poster advertising low-cost medical insurance; on the other side, one selling debt-relief packages. To this poster's left, large windows framed gantries that, since no ferry was docked, were raised. A seagull idled at the end of one. Beneath it, buffers, formed of wooden stakes packed together in tight rows, were turning gangrenous and rotting where they sank into the water. Beyond them, out in the harbour, tankers passed by. I could see one being loaded up over in Red Hook, by giant cranes that looked like insects reared up in the throes of some dying agony. Scanning my gaze across the harbour, to the right, I could see Governors Island, the Statue of Liberty, the outline of New Jersey, with more cranes; then, furthest away of all, no more than a grey lump on the horizon, the place where we were headed.

14.7 The crowd was growing, pressing in now. A lady with a hamburger in her hands bumped me as she went by. The man with the megaphone made his *momentarily* announcement again. On the wall I saw a little screen I hadn't noticed before. It was showing Staten Island attractions: a compilation of vague and generic scenes—people playing golf, or sharing a slap-up meal, or walking through some kind of pleasant-looking shrubbery; a carousel; a football field with children running on it; a man paddling a canoe past reeds and bulrushes. These followed one another in no particular order, then gave over to a picture of an orange ferry cruising through calm waters. Shot (presumably) from a helicopter that circled the moving boat so as to film it from both prow and stern ends and from port and starboard sides as it advanced smoothly and happily across a sea that seemed to welcome it and even help propel it onwards, the scene was idyllic: this bright-orange vessel, cruising through the afternoon, cruising (so it seemed) right out of time, past all statutes and limits, to some other place where everything, even our crimes, has been composted down, mulched over, transformed into moss, pasture and wetland for the duck and coot to build their nests in. Maybe I could somehow nest there too, I told myself; float, calmly, to some spot, some tract from which other terrains might open, realms where everything was different. I turned my head from the screen and looked at the real harbour, the real water. These, with low sunlight bouncing off them, also looked unreal, idyllic. I could make out an actual ferry moving over them towards me: being orange, just like in the film, it seemed to emerge from the bright and hazy light itself, as though the latter's molecules were re-arranging themselves, just like the letters, in an attempt to generate and shape it. Other people had spotted the boat as well: a stir of excitement rippled through the crowd, manifest in hundreds of leg-stances changing, shoulders tightening and lifting, backpacks being slung over backs, general precipitation towards the still-closed sliding doors. Running my gaze once more along the contours of the terminal, I realized that the building was itself shaped like a ferry, its walls angling inwards like a bow as they progressed from north to south, away from the great landmass of Manhattan to the water, the two sides eventually meeting at the sliding doors' flat prow. It struck me that it would have been designed like that, deliberately: a kind of mirror-double of the boats that came to dock at it. As this boat, my boat, loomed nearer, I experienced a vertiginous excitement at the prospect of this happening: a space meeting its inverse, negative and positive coming together, merging into one; and at the prospect of finding myself standing at the very point where this great fusion was occurring. It was more than just a prospect: as the ferry hove still closer, a transfor-mation that was physical seemed to take place; it felt as though not just the ferry but the terminal as well were moving, carry-ing me with it, bearing me onto the verge of something rich, strange and miraculous.

14.8 Gantries were coming down now. People were stream-ing to the doors. The MTA man was announcing, through his megaphone, that the 3:30 ferry had arrived. He repeated the announcement several times. He did this in a ritualized, almost incantatory manner—as though his annunciation of the boat's arrival were a necessary component of the arrival itself, one without which the event could not complete its course. The floor shuddered as the ferry's hull made contact with the buffers. I could make its name out: *Spirit of Change*. Above the writing, in a little cabin topped with radar masts, I could see the captain talking into his radio. Radio-crackle broke out to my right and left: from the MTA man's walkie-talkie, and from those of security personnel scattered about the terminal. It mingled with the crackling of popcorn: several people near me were eating this as they watched the ferry dock, then watched the passengers who'd travelled with it to Manhattan disembark. These arriving passengers looked, in dress and general demeanour, just like the departing ones, but were segregated from the latter by glass walls that led them down a side-tube to the building's exit. Once the last of them had trickled out, the sliding doors opened, and the people thronged around me made towards them.

14.9 I was carried with them, with this throng of people; standing in their midst, I didn't have much choice. Since the terminal was shaped like a big V, the crowd grew more and more compressed the closer to the bottom of this V it moved, like sand-grains running through an hourglass. I tried to recall my flight's departure time; I still had a few more hours. Beyond the glass walls, in the sky, I could see other aeroplanes, all angled sharply up- or downwards as they rose from or descended into Newark. Up or down, whichever direction they had come from or were heading in, their vapour trails all met, again in big *V*s, over Staten Island. They were pointing there; the sky was pointing there; the wind was blowing that way, bearing gliding seagulls down flight-corridors that led there, arranging cloud-wisps into lines that ran along the same paths as the vapour trails. On the ground, flags were straining at their poles in that direction too; all the cranes in Red Hook and New Jersey were angled that way; even the Statue of Liberty pointed towards the grey lump. The mass of people in the terminal started compressing even tighter as the glass walls' funnel grew still narrower, till we became, collectively, a Vanuatan arrowhead, being flighted now across this harbour, on an arced trajectory with the same, inevitable destination, it seemed, as everything else, only a few more feet of terminal and gantry remaining between us and the *pyonngg!* of irreversible release . . .

14.10 I didn't let myself be carried through the doors, though: at the last instant, I held back. This wasn't easy: bodies were wedging me in on all sides. I had to push against them, turn myself around, then hoist and grab at passing arms and shoulders in order to move the other way. At some point, in that final stretch, I'd made my mind up not to take the ferry after all. To go to Staten Island—*actually* go there—would have been profoundly meaningless. What would it, in reality, have solved, or resolved? Nothing. What tangible nesting space would I have discovered there, and for what concrete purpose? None. Not to go there was, of course, profoundly meaningless as well. And so I found myself, as I waded back through the relentless stream of people, struggling just to stay in the same place, suspended between two types of meaninglessness. Did I choose the right one? I don't know. I worked my way out to the side, and stood watching the crowd parading by. Their tight-packedness made them edge and shuffle rather than flow, a stop-start rhythm that was nonetheless placid rather than agitated, their stares fixed not on the back of the person right in front of them (although their eyes all pointed there) but rather on some abstract spot beyond this, or, perhaps, on nothing. The thought struck me that I should be filming this scene on my phone for Daniel, or, perhaps, myself—but I didn't act on this thought. I just stood there, watching. The man on crutches shuffled by; and the one with the wig; and the ones in polyester suits; and the ones in plain, casual clothes. Many had small backpacks, most of which were loose-strung over single shoulders; one young man, though, had a larger one strapped tightly to his back, over both shoulders and around his waist, but hadn't closed it: cloth-like fabric of a fleshy hue was trailing slightly from its unzipped opening. A woman with striped black and yellow shoes edged past me, and for a fleeting instant I thought it was the Minister. It was my jet-lag kicking in, colliding times and places in my head. I saw, amidst the mesh of limbs and torsos, a large bump on someone's neck. I didn't see their face—only their neck, and this just for a second. Helicopters thrummed again; I thought of humming-birds; again a radio crackled, and some children, possibly the ones with the candy-floss, or maybe other ones, processed by. The crowd thinned out; late arrivals scurried past me; then the doors closed; and, almost immediately, the gantries, like the drawbridge to some castle that I'd never enter, were hoisted back up.

14.11 Through the closed doors, their salt-flecked glass, I watched the ship reversing from its berth, churning the water as its hull bumped against the buffers on each side. Once in the open water, it swung round, then made a beeline for the lump on the horizon. Staten Island was no longer grey, and it had grown: the sun was right behind it now, haloing it, transmuting it into a brilliant orange pool that spread across the harbour like a second mass of water, one set on a slightly different plane that spilled across the first one when the two planes intersected. This pool of light was spreading right towards the ferry, swallowing it up, dismantling it pixel by orange pixel. Its haze spread even further, past the boat's still-discernible stern, turning the ferry's wake, and those of other vessels, a metallic, silvery shade. There were scores of wakes, crossing each other in irregular and tangled patterns. *Networks of kinship:* the phrase flashed across my mind; I snorted with derision. Three or four other people who'd been standing in the terminal hadn't taken the boat either. They, like me, stood looking at the harbour, at the light, each other. Were they anthropologists as well? Of course not: the radios of two of them identified them as plain-

clothes security personnel; another was the MTA man, megaphone now hanging at his side. The fourth was a homeless guy
working his way along a row of payphones. That was it: for a
few moments there were just the five of us on the empty concourse, stood (it seemed) in some kind of formal arrangement
whose logic escaped me, amidst discarded popcorn cartons,
like a sparse matinee audience at some movie in which nothing happens. A cleaning machine whined into action, brushes
slowly rotating as it crawled across the floor, squirting disinfec-
tant. Then the first passengers for the next ferry started trickling
in, and the whole cycle started up again.

14.12 I was, as I mentioned, jet-lagged: disorientated, undi-
rected. I'd travelled down to the Staten Island Ferry Terminal
to take the ferry and not taken it, or perhaps just travelled down
there to not take the ferry. I'd been standing in the same spot
for some time now. So, too, had the plain-clothes security
personnel, and the MTA man. As the concourse filled up with
incoming passengers, our arrangement, its sculpted geometry,
which had impressed itself upon me with such clarity and (at
the same time) mystery for a few minutes, faded back into the
general mass of bodies. It was still there, though, camouflaged
or buried: none of us had moved. The homeless guy was still
there, too, going slowly down the row of payphones, searching
for forgotten change caught in their mechanism. In his attempt
to trigger its release, he lifted each receiver from its cradle and
held it up for a few seconds, waiting for coins to drop. None

did. I looked out at the harbour once again. The dazzle on
the water now was all-consuming, overexposed, blinding: the
departed ferry, Staten Island, all the other landmarks and most
of the sky had disappeared in a great holocaust of light, whose
retinal after-effects, in turn, made the terminal's interior too
dark when I turned back to it. It took a few more seconds for
the levels to adjust. I found myself still looking at the homeless
guy. He was still holding a receiver away from his ear, making no attempt to listen to or talk into it. He looked all wrong;
anachronistic. Who uses payphones these days? I wondered
if these ones even worked. I stared at him; our eyes met for a
while; then I, uncomfortable, broke off the contact and started
walking, past the growing stream of people, out of the terminal
and back into the city.

ACKNOWLEDGEMENTS

Satin Island gestated during a 2010 residency at the International Artists Studio Programme in Stockholm, which I spent projecting images of oil spills onto huge white walls and gazing at them for days on end. A year later I was the recipient of equally generous hospitality from the Center for Fiction in New York, who lent me a spacious office in which to sit and think about the general impossibility of writing a novel about the general impossibility of etc. As the book started gathering momentum, Alfie Spencer, Ednyfed Tappy and James Westcott helped it along by giving me an invaluable lid-lift on the strange eddies and cross-currents that arise when the tributaries of left-field thought run into the Amazon of new-corporate culture; to them I'm very grateful. Also to Clementine Deliss, to whom I already owed so much, for showing me her remarkable museum. I should also mention Paul Rabinow, whom I've never met, but whose brilliantly formulated thoughts on the notion of "the contemporary" I have freely and shamelessly lifted. *Satin Island,* like all books, contains hundreds of borrowings, echoes, remixes and straight repetitions. To list them all would take up as much space as the text itself. The critical reader can entertain him- or herself tracking some of them down, if he or she is that way inclined.

Finally, I'm indebted to the point of near bankruptcy to the editorial skills of Alex Bowler at Cape and Dan Frank at Knopf; to Melanie Jackson in New York and Jonathan Pegg in London; and to Eva Stenram everywhere.

A NOTE ABOUT THE AUTHOR

Tom McCarthy was born in 1969 and lives in London. He is known in the art world for the reports, manifestos and media interventions he has made as general secretary of the International Necronautical Society (INS), a semi-fictitious avant-garde network. His previous books include *Men in Space*, *C*, *Remainder* and *Tintin and the Secret of Literature*. In 2013 he was awarded an inaugural Windham-Campbell Literature Prize from Yale University.

A NOTE ON THE TYPE

This book is set in the typeface Tibere, designed by the French typographer Albert Boton. Born in 1932, he began his career as a cabinetmaker, but later apprenticed with Adrian Frutiger in graphic design and worked as a type designer for the Deberny & Peignot type foundry in Paris. Boton has produced numerous well-known typefaces including Brasilia, Eras, and Elan. Tibere is a visually engaging face, distinguished by sharp serifs and terminals, and moderately sized apertures.

Composed by Digital Composition, Berryville, Virginia

Printed and bound by Berryville Graphics, Berryville, Virginia

Designed by Betty Lew